# Trusting Eternity

The Sullivan Vampires, Volume 2

Bridget Essex

## Other Books by Bridget Essex

*Meeting Eternity (Sullivan Vampires, Volume 1)*
*Raised by Wolves*
*Wolf Heart*
*Wolf Queen*
*Falling for Summer*
*The Guardian Angel*
*The Vampire Next Door* (with Natalie Vivien)
*A Wolf for Valentine's Day*
*A Wolf for the Holidays*
*The Christmas Wolf*
*Don't Say Goodbye*
*Forever and a Knight*
*A Knight to Remember*
*Date Knight*
*Wolf Town*
*Dark Angel*
*Big, Bad Wolf*

## Erotica

*Wild*
*Come Home, I Need You*

## About the Author

My name is Bridget Essex, and I've been writing about vampires for almost two decades. I'm influenced most by classic vampires– the vision of CARMILLA (it's one of the oldest lesbian novels!) and DRACULA. My vampires have always been kind of traditional (powerful), but with the added self-torture of regret and the human touch of guilt.

I have a vast collection of knitting needles and teacups, and like to listen to classical music when I write. My first date with my wife was strolling in a garden, so it's safe to say I'm a bit old fashioned. I have a black cat I love very much, and two white dogs who actually convince me to go outside. When I'm actually outside, I begin to realize that writing isn't all there is to life. Just most of it! I'm married to the love of my life, author Natalie Vivien.

The love story of the beautiful but tragic vampire Kane Sullivan and her sweetheart Rose Clyde is my magnum opus, and I'm thrilled to share it with you in ***The Sullivan Vampires*** series, published by **Rose and Star Press**! Find out more at **www.LesbianRomance.org** and **http://BridgetEssex.Wordpress.com**

Trusting Eternity: The Sullivan Vampires, Volume 2

Published by Rose and Star Press
First edition, March 2016



ISBN: 1530409306

ISBN-13: 978-1530409303

# TRUSTING ETERNITY

# DEDICATION

*For the love of my life.*

*And for Marian, who knows the secrets of the Sullivan Vampires, and who loves Tommie as much as I do. Your constant support and love is cherished!*

## -- Eternal Dance --

I was beginning to realize I was having a very, *very* bad day.

I stared at the smug vampire for a long moment. Not that many creatures can pull off smugness as well as a vampire. And Melody was the champion of them all. Her full, red lips glistened as she grinned, folding her arms over her ample chest, throwing back her head so that her rich, red mane spilled out even more impressively over her shoulders.

The poor woman who'd been fiddling with my lock with her screwdriver glanced up with a pained expression. She probably didn't want to be in the middle of what might become a shouting match.

I think Melody wanted me to grovel. She wanted me to beg to stay, to ask for more time, for favors. Maybe she expected me to explode with anger. But I didn't want Melody to have the satisfaction of me losing my temper. I didn't want her to see me reduced to *anything*. So I let out a long, quivering breath, drew myself up to my full height (which wasn't really that impressive, but I liked to think it was made a *little* more impressive by the waves of controlled rage that were emanating from me), and said with a strong, clear voice, "Does Kane know about this?"

A flicker passed over Melody's face just then. It came and went so quickly that I couldn't even be certain that I'd seen it or what, exactly, it was, but then her lips pressed into a firm line. "Yes," she said, drawing out the word into a hiss. "She knows that you need to leave." She straightened and glanced over my shoulder, not meeting my eyes. "Your suitcases have been packed and taken down to the front desk," she told me firmly. "And since your services are no longer required at the Sullivan Hotel, you need to leave." This last part sounded completely triumphant.

My hands balled into fists.

Just like that, the decision had been made for me.

Again.

I was getting a little tired of having my life rearranged by vampires.

"All right," I said, taking a deep breath and trying to hold onto my anger as I considered my rapidly dwindling options, and I began to deflate. My best friend Gwen had driven me here in her beat-up old van, Moochie—so I was without transportation myself. My cell phone was in my room and hadn't been charged in days because I didn't need it that often here. Eternal Cove, the little town in the middle of nowhere where the Sullivan Hotel stood, didn't have a taxi service that I knew of, because it was—of course—a little town in the middle of nowhere.

I needed to talk to Gwen, but I didn't know where to find her.

And I was starting to look like a fool standing my ground where I wasn't wanted.

"All right," I repeated, taking another deep breath. I cleared my throat and thrust my chin forward and up. I would not back down from this woman. Even if she was a vampire. My mind thought furiously, trying to figure out what I could do.

I'd have to walk to town with my cell phone and charger. Go back to the coffee shop Gwen and I had found together. Get the phone charged, call her, ask her to use Moochie to drive me back to New Hampshire. Or maybe I could get a bus ticket…

Either way, it seemed that I was leaving Eternal Cove and all it represented: new life, new chances and choices.

And Kane.

And there was nothing I could do about it.

Anger seethed in my belly. No. There *had* to be something I could do about it. I wasn't going to go down without a fight. This was my new life on the line, my chance at a fresh start. I wouldn't let someone steal it away without giving me a choice.

Okay. First things first. "I need my cell phone," I said clearly, crossing my arms.

Melody tossed my purse at me. "It's all in there," she said with a sweet voice and a wicked smile.

I turned on my heel. I walked quickly back down the steps, anger making my vision cloud to red. I didn't know what to do, but I knew I needed to put some space between myself and the woman—the vampire—who was darkening the glimmer of a good life that had just begun.

I was out in the parking lot before I really came to my senses. I hadn't even had a chance to grab my coat. It was probably already packed in my luggage that had been so unceremoniously hauled to the front desk. Luggage that one person could never possibly carry alone, as my entire life was in those suitcases—or what was left of it. I sighed, rubbing my arms with chilled fingers as I gazed up at the blood-red maples, the brilliant blue sky with the roiling gray clouds on the edge of the horizon, billowing up along the line of the bright ocean. I could see my breath in front of me.

October in New England can be warm and glowing and a brand of gorgeous that can take your breath away—*or* it can be cold and harsh, a type of cold that warns you of the winter yet to come. The latter seemed to be what I was in store for today.

But I was stubborn. I glanced at the Sullivan Hotel behind me and squared my shoulders. The impressive red building sat there, silent and foreboding, without a trace of pity for my human predicament. But I didn't want pity. I didn't want Kane to know how pathetic I was, standing outside of the Sullivan Hotel without a coat or anyplace to go, or—even if I *had* a place to go—transportation to get me there.

I *wasn't* pathetic.

I was going to fix this. No matter what.

I took another deep breath and watched it fog out in front of me. And then I hitched my purse up on my shoulder with numbing fingers, and I marched over the gravel driveway, the little stones crunching beneath my flats, and onto the road just beyond the hedges. The road that sloped down to Eternal Cove.

The town wasn't that far—a few easy, short miles, since it was all downhill, maybe just a little over one mile. I could certainly walk it, and I would have to. But as I began my descent, the chill wind blowing, the cold making my anger turn to ice, I wondered if this was a bright idea.

Let's be honest: I probably should have stayed at the hotel and asked if I could talk to Gwen. It was freezing out; I didn't have my coat… At this point, I was just being stubborn. But I didn't want Melody providing me any "favors."

As I walked along, rubbing at my arms and shivering as the wind picked up in volume, I did my best not to feel sorry for myself. I did my best not to think of Kane or the conversations Melody must have had with her to reach the conclusion that my services were no longer required at the Sullivan Hotel. God, Kane probably *already* thought I was pathetic. She was probably very, very glad that Melody had returned, that I'd been sent away.

But then I'd take another deep breath and remember her cold fingers curling over my hips as her intense blue eyes devoured me, raking over me with a possessive tenderness that took my breath away. Had it only been hours before?

I stood still for a long moment, shaking. I closed my eyes, felt the pavement beneath my flats, felt the wind dancing over my skin, and I remembered Kane's low, husky whisper:

*After all this time, I don't understand what has happened… But what was within Melody that connected me to her... It's gone.*

And then I opened my eyes, staring up at the sky that was almost as violently blue as the vampire's eyes. And I remembered another of her whispers to me:

I am drawn to you. There is something about you that calls to me so strongly I cannot ignore it.

How could I fix this? How could I set things right? Melody had returned, and with her return went every chance I'd ever had with Kane, because everyone knew Melody was Kane's soulmate. She was Kane's *soulmate*, or at least who Kane had professed to be her soulmate. That's the kind of stuff that can't be tampered with, two people so in love that they call each their soulmate.

In that sort of equation, there was no room for anyone else.

Okay. So at this point, I really *was* feeling sorry for myself. As my eyes began to cloud with tears, as I considered what I had just lost, I stood very still on the side of the road, holding my purse's strap with a white-knuckled hand, and holding my side with the other, trying to keep myself from sobbing as the chill wind began to pick up.

And that's when the Mustang came roaring over the hill.

It was probably from the sixties, a type of cherry red they don't make cars in anymore, and I only knew it was a Mustang because of the running horse on the front grill. But it was a very pretty car, regardless of whether I knew cars or not, with its sloping lines and chrome stripes and retro curves. The convertible top was down—unusual on such a cold day—but when I saw who was driving the car, I realized the cold probably didn't bother her very much…since cold didn't seem to bother vampires.

It was Tommie sitting at the wheel, her usually straight, chin-length black hair blowing every which way in the wind her vehicle's passing was creating. She wore slick black sunglasses, and her white dress shirt was unbuttoned at the neck, the bright green tie (that perfectly matched her eyes, I realized) fluttered against that milk-white skin like a beacon.

I never would have been able to notice all those details if she'd just roared right past me. But she didn't. She slowed down her breakneck pace, and she pulled up alongside me, rolling to a complete stop.

She stared at me for a long moment through

her jet-black sunglasses, her mouth—usually contorted into a sexy smirk—frowning, her full lips turning downward.

Tommie sat there, silent.

"I thought vampires didn't like the sunlight," I quipped, which—considering my tear-filled eyes and the circumstances I now found myself in—took a lot out of me to say.

Tommie glanced up at me over the rims of her sunglasses, then, with one brow raised, her head to the side. She leaned forward, her left elbow on the door of her car, her right hand lightly caressing the wheel, her long fingers resting against the leather there.

Tommie was beautiful in a way that engaged my heart in that old cliché: she made my heart skip a beat. From the moment I met her, I'd been attracted to her in that effortless kind of way that pulls you across the room toward another woman, with an invisible tug that you're powerless against, like gravity. She was magnetic: her sarcasm, her laughter that was at once carefree but also hard to find. Tommie smirked quite a bit and could crack a joke about anything, it seemed. But she would never laugh at them.

"What are you doing out here?" she asked heavily, her bright green eyes flashing.

Did she already know that Melody had forced me to leave? Probably. It seemed that news traveled fast in the Sullivan Hotel.

At least, among the vampires.

"I thought I'd get a breath of fresh air," I managed, but it came out a bit choked, and then another tear leaked out of my eyes and ran a bright line down my cheek.

Tommie's jaw clenched, and she breathed out

through her nose, her nostrils flaring as she stared over the edge of her sunglasses, watching the progression of the tear over my skin. She rose in the car, opening the door, her hand gripping the edge of it, her knuckles white. "Let me help you, Rose," she murmured then, the words soft and low and soothing—hypnotic.

My entire body leaned toward her.

I swallowed, tried to control my responses to that low, soothing, sultry voice. "Look," I managed then, anger rising in my belly. I fingered the strap of my purse, trying to clear my head. "That's very…sweet…" I said, gesturing with my hand at the Mustang, at her, with one foot on the ground and one foot still in the car like a woman knight dismounting from her charger. "But I'm not a damsel in distress," I told her with a sad shake of my head. "I don't need to be rescued."

What I didn't say (because I closed my mouth in enough time) was this: I didn't want assistance from any more vampires.

They'd "helped" me quite enough.

"Rose," whispered Tommie then, rising completely, leaving the car door open behind her as she leaned against the side of her Mustang, shrugging out of her sunglasses and peering up at the sun with a long sigh. "You know I'm burning up out here. Maybe I'm the damsel," said Tommie, folding her sunglasses and putting them in her breast pocket of her immaculately white shirt. She stared at me with such an intense gaze, then, that my heart rate skyrocketed. "Maybe I'm in distress," Tommie murmured, her lips twitching at the corners as she carefully controlled her expression.

"Because of a little sunshine?" I asked, glancing upwards. "You're a vampire in the sun. You don't have to be out here," I reminded her gently.

"Maybe I want to be saved," she said, grinning wickedly as she delivered the line with a smoky, low tone that made my toes curl in pleasure. Damn her and her sultry voice. I was supposed to be making my way to a coffee shop and figuring out what I could possibly build out of the newly broken pieces of my life.

Instead, I was standing on the side of a road next to a too-attractive vampire, leaning nonchalantly against a hot red Mustang.

I suppose that, as far as terrible afternoons go, mine was starting to look up.

"See, I want to help. And you're being stubborn," said Tommie, one brow up as her lips twitched at the corners again. She suppressed the smile as she shrugged and folded her arms. "But I can be stubborn, too. Let me help you. Or you're going to be responsible for the serious burns I'll be sporting."

I considered her. "How could you possibly help me?" I asked then, my voice low. I hadn't intended for the words to spill out of my mouth, but then they were there, between us.

Her joking manner was gone in a heartbeat as she leaned forward, pushing off from the side of the car. She was so close to me that I could feel the coolness of her body. Vampires are much colder than the normal human body temperature, I'd learned, and as she took a single step toward me, I could see, again, my breath coming out between us like smoke.

She was so different from Kane as she took my elbow in her sure fingers, coaxing me forward. But different from Kane was...good, right then. I wanted to forget how Kane had held me, how Kane had touched me and kissed me. I wanted to forget the sound of her voice, because all of those memories, the very few that I had of her, were too painful.

But Tommie wasn't like Kane at all. She was a little shorter—though still taller than me. Her body was different from Kane's, more muscular, a little more rakish and boy-like. Kane's long white-blonde hair was nothing like Tommie's short black cut. I wondered what Tommie's hair would feel like in my fingers as the distance between she and me shortened dramatically. Her black hair, as shiny and bright as a raven's wing, seemed like it would be as soft and smooth as ice against my fingers.

Tommie was forward and strong and funny. She was reckless and a little dangerous, I thought.

She was mesmerizing.

Before I knew it, Tommie was standing there—right there. Close enough to lean forward and kiss. Close enough that I could smell the scent of her perfume, something dark, a blend of cologne and organic scents that I couldn't quite place but that made me think of a dress shirt collar, pressed smooth and straight and cool.

Her eyes were hard, bright, the green such a captivating color that I was held spellbound in her gaze as she clenched her jaw and searched my face. Her nose turned up a little at the end, and her full lips were pursed into a frown. They were wet, like she'd just licked them, and my heart began to hammer in my ears.

I wanted to kiss her.

It was a strong and desperate urge that moved through me, but I stomped down on it—hard. I wasn't the type of person to fall for someone who offered me kindness. I was just confused by everything that had just happened and upended my life. Confusion was something I could easily subvert, easily overcome.

I was not going to kiss Tommie Sullivan when, hours before, Kane had held me in her arms.

Tommie watched my face impassively for a moment, and I thought she would say something…but then whatever had risen in her was gone as she straightened, as she stepped away. "Come back with me to the hotel," she said gruffly, running a hand through her hair, which miraculously began to smooth itself down after the ride in the convertible. She held up a hand before I could protest. "You don't have anyplace to go tonight—am I right?" she asked reasonably, her head to the side. I breathed out, my hands curling into fists. It was true, and she knew it, too. "You can talk to Gwen, get something sorted out, make plans—but you can't do anything right now, and you need a place to go, and it's no skin off my back to give you that. It's the least I can do, really," said Tommie, shoving her hands into her dress pants pockets as she shrugged easily, her shoulders curling forward.

"Why?" I breathed out, my breath exhaling into the world like smoke again as I stood my ground, as I held my purse's strap tightly, stood straighter. "Why do you want to help me?" I asked when she turned a little, one brow raised on that perfect face.

"Because," said Tommie softly, sighing, too. "You remind me of someone I used to know."

It was raw, the way she said those words. There wasn't a syllable of sarcasm. But there was a lot of pain.

Tommie straightened the edge of her dress shirt, shrugged her shoulders, the pain rolling away from her as quickly as it'd come.

I trotted around the side of the car, opening the Mustang's heavy door as Tommie hopped in the other side, slamming her door shut and revving the engine with an impish grin on her face.

And we roared back up the hill, toward the Sullivan Hotel.

The gravel spun out from beneath the wheels as we rounded the curve in the road and Tommie all but rammed the car between the hedgerows to get into the parking lot. We skidded to a halt, gravel spraying out in all directions as Tommie cut the ignition and hopped out of the car without opening the door. She smoothly strolled around to the passenger side and opened my door with a low bow and a wide, wry grin.

"Welcome back," she said dryly, straightening as I stood up, glancing back up at the Sullivan Hotel that loomed overhead, staring down at me impassively with its impressive red stone and never-ending array of windows. Behind us, a few more cars were pulling into the almost-full parking lot, too.

In all of the "excitement," I'd forgotten that tonight marked the beginning of the Conference. I didn't know that much about it yet, other than the fact that many of the world's vampires gathered together in one place every year to discuss business, meet and socialize. Every year, a different spot in the world was chosen for the Conference.

And this year, that spot would be the Sullivan Hotel.

As I leaned against the side of the Mustang, the newly-arrived, expensive car had its doors opened, and a few people emerged. One black woman stood straight, tall and as regal as her much-too-pale male companion folded out of the passenger seat. The way these two held themselves, in the slightly old-fashioned dress (the woman wore a very cute retro-looking dress that was red with polka dots and an a-line skirt, and the man looked like he was headed to a costume party as a blonde Dracula), they appeared to me like I'd always imagined vampires would look.

Out of the other expensive car erupted two children who glanced about themselves with feral eyes—a very blonde boy and girl, probably eight years old, wearing jeans and t-shirts and no coats or shoes, even though it was very cold out. A woman rose out of the car after them, possibly their mother. She looked related, at least, with the same feral sheen to her eyes as she watched them running around in the parking lot. She wore jeans, too, and she barked at the kids to follow her.

Maybe it was their eyes or the way they looked at me as they ran past me—like they'd missed lunch, and I might make a very tasty snack—but I realized right away that the kids were probably not human.

"Vampire…*children*?" I managed, glancing sidelong at Tommie, who smiled widely, shoving her hands into her pockets as she rolled her shoulders back.

"Why not?" she asked me, cocking her head as she glanced after the kids. "Those two, though—they're the stuff of nightmares. Timmy and Tammy. Stay away from them. They're pretty bloodthirsty and…have gotten into a little bit of trouble because of it, at past Conferences."

I watched the savage children scamper up the few steps, through the blood-red columns and into the Sullivan Hotel itself, the massive doors opening and shutting behind them as Tommie cleared her throat, standing a little straighter as she glanced up at the dark shadows along the edge of the horizon, a big cloudbank that looked dark and gray and threatening as it started to drift closer to us, beginning to block out the bright blue sky.

"It's going to storm soon," she remarked mildly. But a shiver ran through me, nonetheless. Her words seemed like a particularly poignant omen. Not only of what was to come here, but of my life, in general.

I didn't know yet how right she was.

Another car pulled in—the parking lot was starting to get busier and busier, what with the Conference beginning tonight. This one was a smaller European car, all bold lines with a bright lime-green exterior. The woman who stepped out of it had heels that would probably have killed a normal mortal woman on the gravel ground, and a bright pink skirt so short that I couldn't help but stare at her legs. Long, wavy blonde hair reached down to the middle of her back, and she glanced over the tops of her sunglasses in our direction before taking the glasses off, a wide grin making her full, red lips curl up very prettily at the corners.

"Tommie!" she called, and her voice was so warm, her expression so bright and kind, that I couldn't help but like her almost immediately. She trotted across the rest of the parking lot toward us as Tommie returned her grin, stepping forward to embrace her tightly. Tommie squeezed so forcefully that she almost picked the stranger up off the ground.

"Francesca, how long has it been?" asked Tommie, one of the first looks of real pleasure I'd ever seen on her face deepening as she stepped back and held the laughing woman at arm's length. Tommie looked genuinely glad to be in this stranger's company.

"Oh, about fifty years, give or take?" the blonde laughed, raising one brow imperiously as she shoved her sunglasses into the little teal clutch dangling at her wrist. She smoothed the lapel of her bright blue jacket, turning to look at me with another warm smile. She was more beautiful than a model, but she was so down to earth, too, as she held out a perfectly manicured hand to me—nails colored the same teal as her clutch. "I'm Francesca Muldoon, but everyone close to me calls me Frank," she winked impishly and glanced at Tommie with one brow raised. "Are you a...*friend*...of Tommie's?"

The way she said "friend" could really have implied only one thing. I turned bright red and shook my head—a little too quickly, as Tommie frowned and cleared her throat.

"No... Rose was hired on as an employee of the Sullivan Hotel," said Tommie smoothly. "She's just a friend."

"It's hard for you to have women as 'just' friends, Tommie. If I recall correctly," said Frank, drawing herself up to her full height, which her desperately tall heels only emphasized.

"Well, it's been a long time," said Tommie, and they weren't sharp, those words. They were almost sad and small. "Anyway," said Tommie with a shrug, her smile returning as she took Frank's elbow with sure fingers. "We have a lot of catching up to do, don't we?"

"It'll be like old times. I'm really glad I came to this Conference after missing so many of the others. I've missed you," said Frank with a warm smile. "And it'll be nice to get to know you, Rose," said Frank, as she turned to wink at me.

I began to smile, too.

And that's when another car pulled into the parking lot.

Cars kept coming. It wasn't unusual that one chose that heartbeat to pull in. But there was something about it. My skin shivered as the shiny black thing—a sports car of some kind with all sorts of chrome—pulled into a spot right next to Tommie's Mustang.

The ignition shut off, the car door swung open as if shoved, and impressively tall high heels and curving feet came out first.

And Mags rose up and out of the car.

She didn't take off her sunglasses, but I could tell instantly the expression of loathing that passed over her face as she stared at me. Really, what had I ever done to her to make her hate me so much? Hate me enough, in fact, to try to drink me dry? Mags said not a word as she shut the car door with her hip, making the close-fitting dress wiggle impressively as she shimmied over the ground to stand next to Tommie. Ignoring Francesca and me entirely, Mags put her arms around Tommie's neck.

And Mags curled her fingers with their bright red tips into Tommie's hair, something only a lover would dare, and drew Tommie forward for a hard, harsh kiss.

Francesca glanced down at her purse, her mouth in a thin, hard line, as I felt the heat rise into my cheeks. Mags backed away from Tommie after a long moment, her perfect lipstick smudged onto the side of Tommie's mouth. Tommie's eyes were like stones as she glanced at Mags, as she carefully took a handkerchief out of her dress pants pocket and wiped at the smudged lipstick on her pale skin.

"Aren't you back a little early?" is what Tommie said to Mags then, tiredly.

Mags had been sent away from the Sullivan Hotel for a week in "punishment"—because of the fact that she tried to kill me. A fact that I was acutely aware of as Mags turned to me, glanced at me, both brows lifted up imperiously over her sunglasses, before she turned back to Tommie, shaking her head.

"I've done my time," she said, snarling over that last word. "And for what? I heard she's leaving, after all." Mags glanced at me as if I was a stain on one of her very impressive dresses. "Tommie, baby, we have a lot to catch up on," she said, her voice practically purring as she threaded her arm, snake-like through Tommie's. "Let's go somewhere…" she said, stepping forward so that the front of her body was pressed tightly against Tommie's, her round, full breasts shoved forcefully against Tommie's almost-flat chest. "Let's go somewhere where we can be alone," she breathed.

"I'll see you later, Tommie," said Francesca, her words soft as she took a step backward.

"No," said Tommie resolutely, taking a step backward, too—moving away from Mags. "We have a lot of catching up to do, Frank…and we have things to discuss, Rose. Mags, I can't talk right now," she murmured, her voice dropping soft and low as she glanced at the sultry woman with something akin to regret.

If Mags was offended at Tommie's dismissal, she didn't show it. Her head moved dangerously to the side, like a bird of prey getting ready to size up a kill, and then she straightened, her mouth forming a slow, sensuous smile. "Maybe later," she murmured, her bright pink tongue licking her lips languorously before she turned on her heel, her hips moving hypnotically beneath the skirt of her dress, causing all of our eyes to watch her until she'd gone up the few steps and onto the front veranda of the Sullivan Hotel, and then through the front door, disappearing from view.

"Well, Mags certainly hasn't changed much," Frank remarked wryly, shaking her head and clicking her clutch shut as she rolled her eyes a little.

"You'd be surprised," Tommie muttered, glancing sidelong at me. "She tried to drain Rose."

"Like I said," Frank muttered, thumbing the pack of cigarettes she'd dredged out of her clutch. She shook out one and held it easily, unlit between her first two fingers.

Far out over the sea, a flicker of lightning touched down into the water, so distant that it looked like static electricity. It was followed by a very distant roll of thunder.

"Let's get inside," Tommie remarked, gesturing forward. She hopped back into her car for a moment, starting the engine and making the convertible's top roll up. The first big, fat drops of rain splattered against her windshield as Frank and I trotted toward the front door of the Sullivan Hotel, Tommie on our heels.

We got underneath the veranda's roof as the sky opened up.

"Perfect weather for a Conference," Frank murmured happily as we watched the rain pounding against the gravel parking lot. There were a few more headlights pulling into the lot, and a few more guests running for cover and the front door. The rain was so cold, and as I stared out at the parking lot, at the men and women with umbrellas or coats over their heads, moving past us and through the door, which kept opening and shutting, making the laughter and voices inside muted or loud as it opened and closed, I realized that I would probably still have been on the road to town with the heavens pouring rain upon me if Tommie hadn't come and brought me back here. I probably would have caught my death of cold. At the very least, I would have been freezing and alone and miserable.

I chanced a sidelong glance at Tommie, who had her arms folded, her legs hip-width apart, and her nose up as she stared out at the rainstorm. If she had similar thoughts to mine—that maybe she really *was* my lady knight in shining armor—she didn't voice them, or make any expressions to suggest as much.

Tommie was very beautiful in that eerie half-light of the thunderstorm, with her proud face pointed up at the heavens and her unreadable expression, as if her mind were a million miles away. But Tommie turned then, catching the door as another vampire woman strode through it, and she held the door for both Francesca and me as we entered the Sullivan Hotel together.

Since it was starting to get dark, all of the ornate, art-deco wall lamps were on inside, their brass fixtures shining warmly in the low light. To combat the creeping darkness in the wide hallway, all of the art lamps above the paintings in the main hall of the hotel were turned on. The sumptuous blood-red and black marble floor tiles were wet in spots from the rain that dripped from the guests, as the vampires removed their coats and began to mill about in—what I realized—was a beginning reception of sorts.

Old oaken tables had been set up along the wall, beneath the paintings, and on top of the antique lace tablecloths, there were many pretty wine stems and liquor glasses lined up—as well as many, many, *many* multicolored bottles of booze.

It almost looked like a normal, fancy reception. Save for one thing:

There was not a bite to eat.

I mean, it was a meeting of *vampires*: The fact that that there was no food really wasn't that surprising. I was surprised a little, though, that they drank liquor.

I glanced at the front desk, at my coworker—or, rather, I supposed…my ex-coworker—Clare, perched on a stool behind the desk. She didn't exactly look afraid, but there was something odd about her body language, her hands folded, knuckles white, on her lap, her blue tartan skirt tucked tightly beneath her, as if she was cold, as she stared at the vampires milling in front of her with wide eyes.

I wondered if the main course wasn't visible because it wasn't something you could put on a table.

I wondered if it was, rather, some*one*.

It was a chilling thought, a thought I'd been trying to ignore, considering the fact that vampires from all over the world were congregating before my very eyes. Vampires who, by their very nature, craved human blood. The only thing that made me feel a little safe was the fact that Kane, and the other Sullivans, had mentioned that they ignored the more bloodthirsty aspects of vampirism as a group.

However, the same could not necessarily be said for the rest of the vampires here, and I had a feeling that the Sullivans were likely a rarity among vampires.

I mean…it was the thing vampires were known

for, wasn't it? Drinking blood?

At this point, I hadn't learned that much about vampires. I knew that they lived a long time and were incredibly strong and magnetic. I knew that they craved human blood but could live without it if they chose to do so. I knew that they probably didn't sleep in coffins but that sunlight burned them badly over time. I knew little else.

But as I stared at this group of beautiful creatures milling about, drinking champagne out of thin, expensive glasses with blood-red lips and laughing with lovely voices in the hallway as the rain poured down outside, I knew that, as a human being, I'd willingly walked into a proverbial lions' den.

Mags, chuckling with a tall, red-headed man in a dark suit over flutes of champagne, turned to glance over her shoulder at me just then.

Her wicked, terrifying smile included sharp, glittering fangs.

If she was trying to frighten me…she'd done a pretty good job of it. But I was more stubborn than that. Right now, I didn't have anyplace to go. And if I'd learned anything about Kane, it was this:

We were safe in the Sullivan Hotel. No matter who stayed here.

Mags had attacked me in the water, down on the beach. And even then, somehow, impossibly, Kane had saved my life. Somehow, she'd known I was in distress. I wasn't certain of the rules and restraints of the vampires' Conference, but I was almost certain that Kane had put something in place to protect the humans in her care.

As if my thoughts themselves had summoned her, there she was then, across the room.

Her long, white blonde hair was swept back from her face and fell like a cascade of satin over her shoulders, and she wore a shirt in the most appropriate shade of red for a vampire. It had a surprisingly plunging neckline, and her bare skin above her breasts was covered in dripping black gems fashioned in an elaborate, decadent necklace. There was a tall black collar on her black jacket, and if my eyes weren't mistaken in the dim lighting, she also wore leather pants that seemed to have been made perfectly for her body, like a second skin, and a pair of tight-fitting leather boots with thick black heels.

I reached out to steady myself with a hand against the corner of the wall. Not because she was beautiful in a way that made my knees weak—though she was—but because, in the space between us, a…line seemed to pulse. It's the best way I can describe it.

It was as if a glowing thread was tied around my heart, stretched across the distance between us, and was tugging at Kane's heart, too.

I knew without a shadow of a doubt in that moment that we were inextricably linked. Connected, utterly.

If Kane felt that connection, that bright pull from that invisible thread, I couldn't say…because it wasn't me that her powerful blue eyes found.

Kane's eyes found Mags and pinned the woman beneath her gaze.

Mags stopped speaking to her male companion. Across the crowded room, she lifted her champagne flute to Kane in a mocking sort of toast and drained the contents dry in a single swallow. She kept her eyes trained on Kane's as Kane stalked her way across the room, threading herself between the assembled vampires—or maybe they parted for her so that she could move easily and quickly across the crowded room—to reach Mags.

I couldn't hear what the two women said to one another as Kane inclined her head toward Mags, as they stepped so close to one another, it looked like a fight was about to begin, their stares so hard and intense—nose to nose. Both Kane and Mags' eyes were flashing as Kane turned, indicating the corridor with a quick hand. Mags didn't look at Kane as she sailed past her, nose up, fangs bared in a snarl.

And Kane and Mags left the room together, speaking heatedly and quietly as they both stalked down the corridor.

Was Kane talking to Mags about…me? Maybe it was absurd to think that I mattered so much to Kane—after all, hadn't I been discharged from the Sullivan Hotel without any interference from her? But there had been something in the clenching of Kane's jaw, and the dangerous glittering of Mags' eyes…

I thought that, yes, maybe they were talking about the incident that had garnered Mags' "punishment." Though I did not—and still don't—think leaving the Sullivan Hotel for a week is an appropriate sentence for *attempted murder.* Maybe vampires simply think about things differently, I mused as I stood there, one hand still against the wall, the other over my heart to quell its incessant beating. How much did one human life count to a being who considered us…dessert?

But that was unfair. Kane had never thought of me that way, I knew. Though I wondered, then, if what I'd felt between us had really been that special, after all. I was trying to heal the hurt in my heart. I knew better.

But I was trying to convince myself otherwise.

But how could I explain that pulsing connection between Kane and me that I had just felt? Honestly, I'd never felt anything like it before in my entire life. It was otherworldly, that tug that had compelled me to lean toward her amidst the crowd. It was nothing I could explain—but it had been there, all the same.

Across the room, then, I saw Melody. Her bright red hair was unbound and hung down around her shoulders in satin waves. She was wearing a red dress with a plunging neckline—so plunging, in fact, that the neckline itself ended somewhere around her navel, her breasts hardly concealed by scallops of red fabric. She was laughing at something a dark-haired woman was saying, the woman bending her head to speak into Melody's ear. And as Melody lifted up her gaze, ready to retort something to her companion…she saw me.

She looked surprised and genuinely confused for a heartbeat.

And then unmistakable rage passed over her face, contorting her pretty mouth into a snarl before she turned away, lowering her voice and speaking again to her companion.

This wasn't a good idea.

I didn't want a scene; I didn't want to be made a fool of in front of all these people. I probably shouldn't have come back to the Sullivan Hotel, but Tommie had been convincing, and…I had no place else to go.

Tommie was at my elbow, then, her sure, strong fingers gripping me gently, curling over my skin. "Let's go up to my rooms," she said in a low voice, her lips close enough to my ear that I felt them brush against my skin. I shivered at that unexpected touch. But there was a thin shiver of delight that raced through me, too.

I turned to glance up at Tommie. Having just seen Kane, having just felt that bright thread of connection pulsing between us…I knew that I didn't have that same sensation with Tommie. Between Kane and me ran an electric thread. It was something extraordinary.

But there was a deep attraction between Tommie Sullivan and me, and there was absolutely no denying that fact.

Still, it didn't matter. None of this mattered. Because now that we were back at the Sullivan Hotel, I could find Gwen, and she and I could figure out how to get me back to New Hampshire. Where I'd start my life fresh, free of a strange, glittering, beautiful life full of vampires.

"What about your friend?" I asked, nodding in the direction of Francesca, whose head was bent to a beautiful female vampire with jet black, straight hair who was whispering into her ear. They looked intimately acquainted, the way this vampire laid a hand on Francesca's pink-clad hip.

"There's time enough for that—and anyway, she looks…occupied," said Tommie with a shake of her head. Then, her fingers still wrapped strong and gentle around my arm, we walked down the corridor, in the opposite direction that Kane and Mags had taken.

"I need to speak with Gwen," I told Tommie once we'd reached the bottom of the spiral staircase; we'd gotten here, walking the entire five minutes, in silence. We paused next to the first wide step of the staircase, and I gazed up at Tommie's face. She had a carefully schooled expression of neutrality as she shrugged.

"I don't know where Gwen is right now. Why don't you call her?"

I blushed, biting my lip. "My cell phone is dead," I told her.

"You can charge it in my room—and you must be hungry," Tommie noted, her head to the side. "I can get food for you, bring it up to you. I don't want Melody to see you," she murmured, stepping closer.

"It's too late for that," I murmured back, glancing over Tommie's shoulder at the empty corridor behind us. I shivered a little beneath her intense gaze, her green eyes flashing. "Melody already saw me—at the reception."

"Well," said Tommie, working her jaw as she glanced up at the staircase. "Let's get to my rooms. Just…in case."

"In case of what?" I asked, another shiver moving over my skin.

Tommie paused, her foot on the first step, her fingers still wrapped around my arm. She let me go. "Melody isn't really…how she used to be," said Tommie, shaking her head, not meeting my gaze. "She's not how she was when I knew her. Before. She's…very different."

The words sounded so forlorn, so remorseful. I paused for a long moment, watching Tommie climb the steps.

"You knew Melody before she…died?" I asked her, then. My words sounded strange to my ears as I began to climb after her.

"We all did," Tommie answered, walking slowly up the steps, her long fingers trailing on the railing.

"Some…better than others."

Now her words sounded bitter. I tried to put the pieces together. Tommie's shoulders were rigid, and she hadn't been sarcastic *once* since we'd entered the building.

"Did you see Kane—" I began, but Tommie rounded on me, glaring down at me for a long moment with a shake of her head.

"I saw Kane with Melody," she whispered, the words low and growling. "Together."

For a long moment, I stood very still.

And then it dawned on me.

"Were you in love with Melody?" I asked.

Tommie paused on the steps, her back to me. Her shoulders relaxed.

"Yes," she said simply. I caught up with her on the wide staircase, and we both shared the same step, somewhere between the second and third landing. Tommie cast a sidelong glance my way, and her eyes were shining in the half-light. Bright with tears, I realized, as she shook her head, breathed out, biting her lower lip and glancing up at the landing. "I loved her very much," she said then, her words soft and vulnerable—so unlike the wry, assured Tommie I'd experienced in the short time I'd known her. She sighed, not wiping the tear away as it leaked out of her right eye, tracing a line down her face. She stood straighter.

We climbed the rest of the steps, and Tommie took her landing with a long stride, her hands deep in her dress pants pockets. "It's not as if it was some sweeping love story," Tommie choked out, rolling her wet eyes. "I didn't have a chance with Melody," she said over her shoulder, her mouth twisted into a grimace. "Kane and Melody... That was a connection that nothing could break. I didn't have a chance, but sometimes you love people you know you can't be with, because you're just powerless against it. That's how it was with Melody and me. I was powerless against it. Against her. I loved her, and I couldn't *stop* loving her."

It was a poignant, beautiful speech—and I could understand it on a human level. But I thought about the Melody downstairs, the Melody I knew. It was hard for me to believe that anyone could love *that* woman so much, let alone the two women I'd been attracted to at the Sullivan Hotel. How could *Kane* and *Tommie* love her so much and so fiercely? Kane and Tommie were very different, it was true, but they had some things in common. They were both incredibly self-assured and knew exactly what they wanted. They were strong, independent and fierce... What could women like that possibly see in petulant, cruel Melody?

As if Tommie could hear my thoughts, she shook her head as we walked down this new corridor, her shoes clicking against the blood-red and black tiles. I hadn't been paying attention to which landing we'd gotten off on, but I figured we must be on the floor on which the Sullivan Vampires had their quarters. The doors were ornately carved, and the windows had heavy, black curtains drawn over them.

"Melody wasn't always like this. How you know her," said Tommie softly, quietly. "She wasn't like this at all," she whispered. "She was..." Her voice trailed off as she paused before a tall, mahogany door carved with grapevines. She fished her key ring out of her pocket. "She was very kind. Very gentle. She made you forget everything dark and terrible that you'd ever seen." Tommie was gazing at the door as if she could see right through it, her eyes unfocused…gazing back on the past. "She had a laugh that was bright, like sunshine. She was thoughtful. She remembered things you said—little things, things that weren't of any consequence, and she'd do something about them. Fix them. One time she learned that I'd lost my hat in a fall from my horse. This is way back in the day," said Tommie, her mouth quirking up at the corners as she remembered. "She went out and bought me a new hat, and brought it to me. 'Just like the ones you love wearing,' she said. I remember that. It…touched me," said Tommie, her voice going low again as she gazed down at the doorknob while she fit the key into the lock. "Honestly," said Tommie, then, over her shoulder, "Melody reminded me of you."

Startled, I stood there for a long moment in the corridor, closing and opening my fists. I thought about what Tommie had said. It would have been the most terrible of insults if Tommie had compared me to the Melody downstairs.

But the Melody she'd known once…she didn't sound like the newfound Melody.

Not at all.

"Isn't that strange," I offered, following Tommie into the room as I glanced about. "How time can change someone so much."

"That's like a line from 'Unchained Melody', isn't it?" said Tommie, her mouth quirking sideways as she took a hat off the elaborately carved coat rack by the front door and plunked it on her head. It was a fedora with a black satin ribbon looping around it. She sprawled down in a plush blue chair by the unlit fireplace as she stretched overhead.

The rooms I now found myself in were what I

might have described as masculine if I hadn't known a woman lived in them. They were very sparse and furnished with only a few choice pieces of furniture. There was the main room, with a couch and chairs, a smaller room to the left that looked like a miniature library, the walls lined with mahogany shelves filled with messy rows of books, and then the bedroom to the right. All of the walls in the rooms were covered with the same blue wallpaper and were mostly bare. Coupled with the few, modern-looking pieces of furniture, Tommie's living quarters gave me a Spartan feel, as if every object within them had to have a purpose or would not be permitted within these rooms.

The bed in the room to the far right was the only beautiful thing here, a sprawling king-size bed with a headboard and footboard made out of a dark, well-polished antique wood carved with vines and flowers. The bed looked tall enough that you might need a stool to climb up into it.

"Impressed?" Tommie remarked, her mouth curling in a wry smile as she caught me glancing into her bedroom.

I was appalled to find myself blushing as I shook my head, turning away from her and hoping my hair covered my red cheeks. I suddenly realized that an incredibly attractive woman—who I was incredibly attracted *to*—was lounging in a chair very close to me. The blush deepened as Tommie stood, her mouth now grinning wickedly as her gaze raked over me.

"Are you comfortable here, Rose?" she asked then, her voice neutral but low and sultry enough to send a shiver down my spine.

"Yes," I told her, which was a sort-of truth. I glanced up at her quickly, taking my purse off my shoulder. "I…I have to plug in my phone," I stammered, trying to open the zipper on the purse and fumbling with it. I quietly cursed myself at being so clumsy.

I wasn't special. Heaven knows that Tommie would probably have put the moves on a female statue. It wasn't particular *special* that she leaned closer to me then, her fingers curling around my waist…to take the purse from me. She grinned deeper as I let out a sigh while she brushed past me, her hip bone grazing mine with a soft nudge as she took my phone and its charger out of my purse, tossing the purse back onto the chair she'd vacated. She crouched down next to the side of the fireplace, plugging the charger into the wall.

"Thank you for helping me, Tommie," I whispered.

Tommie glanced up quickly at that, shaking her head as she plugged my phone into the charger. It beeped but didn't light up in her hand.

"It's no trouble," she said tiredly, setting the phone down onto the floor as she placed an elbow on one knee, glancing up at me. I was suddenly aware of how stunning she looked, kneeling on one knee like someone preparing to be knighted. I audibly gulped as she rose smoothly, shaking her head. "It's the least I can do, really," she told me, putting her hands in her pockets after a long moment, leaning forward toward me. She straightened a little, shaking her head. "Anyway, I can go get you food—you must be hungry. I'll have to leave you here. And you'll have to stay out of sight, sadly, what with Melody and Mags—"

"Tommie." I don't know why I thought of it at that moment, but I'd been wondering, and, given that this would probably be my last night here, I might as well ask. "Are you and Mags..." I trailed off, remembering Mags' passionate kiss upon greeting Tommie.

"We're friends with very few benefits," said Tommie, then, one brow up. "Does that bother you?"

"Of course not," I told her quickly.

"Ah. Well," said Tommie, striding smoothly in front of me as she curled her fingers over my hips again. Two hands against my hips held me snugly against her as my heart hammered, as I stared up at her open-mouthed. "Why did you ask?" whispered Tommie, her bright green eyes staring down and into me.

She felt strange against me. Her body was hard in a way that Anna's had not been, harder than Kane's. Kane had fit against me in all the right places, and Tommie didn't exactly do that—we didn't join, curve to curve, effortlessly. But do you need to? Isn't connection, a body against a body, enough?

I was so confused as I looked up at Tommie. I wasn't entirely certain if I wanted this. We can be attracted to anyone and everyone, but acting on that attraction is another matter entirely.

But it's not as if Kane and I were together, or would ever be together, now that Melody was in the picture. I wasn't cheating or doing something wrong if I kissed this woman. And I did desperately want to kiss her, to put my arms around her, to drag her down to me and taste her. The attraction, the want, burned through me like my blood, rushing and moving much too quickly.

Still, I knew, in that moment, that what I did now would matter.

And that made me pause.

I was angry at myself. I wasn't with Kane. It was over. I should just kiss Tommie, should let things go wherever they were headed. I wasn't like this, usually, but I was hurt, and I needed something soft and nice and lovely. And Tommie didn't fit that longing entirely—she wasn't soft or nice, but she certainly was lovely. And she was nice to me, I supposed. That counted for something.

I wanted to stop thinking, to stop weighing everything, the good and the bad, to stop wishing for something that would never be.

So I closed my eyes as I lifted up my face, as Tommie bent down to me. And as effortless as breathing, our mouths connected.

She was cold, her mouth chill against my lips as I kissed her, but it was a pleasant chill, the kind that sends a shiver down your spine, the kind you can taste, like bright mint or the taste of the first snowfall, slightly metallic. Almost immediately it was a hard kiss, a desperate sort of kiss, as I wrapped my arms around her neck, and her fingers dug into my hips, hard.

Then somehow, terribly, there was a knock at the door.

Tommie didn't pause in her kiss, only pressed me harder to her, but I took a step back, my hands on her chest now as I glanced backward.

"Leave it," Tommie growled softly, almost inaudibly, as she stared down at me with bright, savage eyes.

"Miss Sullivan? I'm sorry to disturb you. It's me—Gwen," said Gwen on the other side of the door.

Tommie sighed, then, sliding her hands over me as she took a step back, raking her fingers through her hair. She shrugged. "Just a minute," she muttered loudly, then cleared her throat, looking to me as she raised a single brow and crossed her arms over her chest.

I cleared my throat, too, my hands rising up to my hair. But nothing had happened. We'd just kissed. I pressed my fingers to my lips—they'd probably be bruised in the morning. I probably *looked* freshly kissed.

But that was okay. It was just Gwen at the door. Gwen would understand.

And I shouldn't feel guilty about *anything*. Because there was nothing between Kane and me.

I was beginning to realize that there never had been.

I squared my shoulders, walked to the door and opened it.

Gwen's eyes became round as she glanced from me to Tommie, further back in the room. "Hi… I'm sorry to disturb you?" she asked, her head to the side. Whether she was wondering if she was sorry or if she'd actually disturbed us, I wasn't sure, but a smile flickered across Gwen's face before she tilted her head to the side, folding her arms. "Um…Rose?"

I shook my head, bit my lip and went back into the room to retrieve my purse, to remove my cell phone charger out of the wall and take my phone. It hadn't been long enough for the phone to charge, but I needed to talk to Gwen now. "Thank you for your help," I told Tommie, pausing in the doorway for a long moment.

She shrugged elegantly, leaning against the wall as she watched me go, her expression unreadable. "I hope I'll see you sooner rather than later," is all she said to me.

And there was regret in her voice and her eyes

as I shut the door behind me.

"So…there's a lot going on, and I don't know if I have the story straight or…what the heck just happened?" asked Gwen as we began to stride quickly down the corridor, her voice rising in an excited squeak. "Oh, my God, were you just making out with Tommie Sullivan?"

I grinned in spite of myself, shaking my head. But then the gravity of my situation came back to me. "I mean, yes—but there are more pressing matters, Gwen. I was let go from the Sullivan Hotel. Fired. It's over."

She paused, the glee in her face dissolving to worry. "What? Why? Who—"

"Melody fired me. And for no reason—no *real* reason, anyway. I think she did it because…she feels threatened by me? Because she thinks that there's something between me and Kane?" I spread my hands and shook my head. "But, regardless, I'm no longer an employee of the Sullivan Hotel. The lock was changed on my room, and Melody technically kicked me out this morning. My suitcases are down at the front desk. She wants me gone. But I don't have a car…" I trailed off, shaking my head in frustration as I sighed out. "I just don't really know what to do."

"Have you talked to Kane about this?" Gwen's voice was low, a whisper, as I glanced up at her quickly. She shook her head. "Don't give me that look," she continued, hands on her hips now as she glared at me. "*Did* you?"

"Melody told me that Kane agreed with her decision to dismiss me," I said, but my words sounded weak and flat, even to my own ears. Melody hadn't said exactly that. Melody had said that Kane *knows that you need to leave.*

"Screw Melody. I *really* think you should go and talk to Kane about this," Gwen urged. She glanced down at the slim silver watch on her wrist. "It's almost six o'clock…" She nudged aside one of the thick black curtains over a floor-to-ceiling-length window—outside, it was already dim and twilit, the parking lot far below, the ocean and the glimmering, distant lights of Eternal Cove all washed in monochrome. The storm raged on with rain pelting the window with a curtain of rough water. "I have to get into my cocktail uniform," said Gwen, closing the curtain snugly again. "The Conference begins tonight with 'an intimate party in the Sullivan drawing room,' and I'll be there—serving cocktails to everyone," she said, hurrying along the corridor. She glanced over her shoulder at me. "Promise me you'll talk to Kane? I really think we can get this sorted out," said Gwen, as I hurried after her.

"I don't know if it'll be that easy," I warned, but her calm confidence in the situation made me feel better about it. I was very glad, again, that Tommie hadn't let me walk all the way to Eternal Cove, where I would have waited for hours by myself, getting more depressed by the moment over my new lot in life.

The afternoon had certainly taken a different direction than I ever could have predicted.

A much better direction—I hoped.

"Of *course* it'll be that easy," said Gwen smoothly. We'd reached the spiral staircase, and we began to head up it to the fifth floor. Gwen, who was already on the staircase ahead of me, glanced down at me with a small, calm smile. "Honestly, Rose, this is just a minor roadblock; it's completely fixable. I really believe you were meant to be here."

Her words made me stop cold, one hand on the banister, the other brushing frozen fingertips against the fabric of my skirt. "Why do you… Why do you say that?" I managed, glancing up at her.

She shrugged, shaking her unruly mane. Curls flew every which way as her brow furrowed, her hand spinning a low, lazy circle as she tried to figure out what to say. "You know how you just *know* something?" she asked me, her head to the side. "I've known that you were meant to be here. Hell, I've felt that way ever since I arrived. There was a Rose-shaped hole in the Sullivan Hotel long before you ever got here. And now it's been filled. And it can't go back to being empty." Gwen's smile at me radiated confidence, and I followed my best friend up the stairs with slow, plodding steps, mystified.

Gwen's the kind of woman who believes in angels and crystals and past lives and cosmic energy, the kind of woman who trusts the universe because it's got something wonderful in store for her.

I've never been that kind of woman. I've never had that kind of trust.

But when Gwen said, just then, that I was meant to be at the Sullivan Hotel…I felt the rightness of those words, too.

Because I'd felt the same way, when I first arrived.

I'd known I was meant to be here.

We climbed to the fifth floor and strode to Gwen's door, situated right next to mine, with its shiny new doorknob and lock glittering in the overhead lights. I sighed unhappily, glancing at it, but Gwen shook her head as she slipped her own key into her lock and turned the door handle. She pushed the door open and stepped inside her room. "Seriously, don't you worry about that. We're going to fix this. Don't worry, okay?" she said with her brows raised.

Gwen tossed her key ring onto the bed and picked up a long dry-cleaning bag that had been hung on a wall hook. "I have to get changed super fast, or I'm going to be late." Then she trotted into the bathroom and partially shut the door behind her with her hip. "So, Tommie?" she called out, utterly relentless.

I grinned in spite of myself, glancing at my reflection in the antique silver mirror above the dresser. If I'd looked freshly kissed before when Gwen had first seen me, I didn't now, but the memory of Tommie's mouth on my own lingered on my lips. I reached up and touched my mouth with my fingertips, watching my reflection, watching my eyes. They were hooded, unreadable, though my smile certainly said a lot.

"Yeah?" I called to Gwen, and sat down on the bed, leaning back on my hands after I plunked my purse down beside me, my cell phone and my charger spilling out of it.

"I thought you told me you were attracted to *Kane*? That you weren't attracted to Tommie because you wanted a relationship…and that you were *pretty* certain that Tommie was incapable of having a relationship—if I recall correctly." Her tone was wheedling, and I could hear zippers being sworn at under her breath. I shook my head, glancing down at my shoes. I kicked off my flats, let my feet rest against the cool wood floor absentmindedly.

"I'm still not certain how capable Tommie *is* of a relationship," I said softly, and I paused, considering Gwen's words. "But…but maybe *I'm* not in the market for a relationship right now."

There was a strangled sound, and then Gwen peered around the door with wide eyes. "Rose Clyde, are you telling me that you're looking for a one-night stand?"

Gwen sounded half-joking and half in shock as she pushed the bathroom door open the entire way, fiddling with the back of her tiny dress. She didn't give me a chance to reply. "Can you help me with this *stupid* dress? It's so annoying, and I'm so *late*," she moaned, turning her back to me and showing me the half-zipped-up zipper.

"Wait—you're *wearing* that?" I gasped incredulously.

Gwen looked, well…hyper-sexualized. She was wearing a short maid's outfit, complete with a fluffy black skirt that only *just* covered her bottom, tons of tulle and a white lacy apron. Her black stockings sheathed the skin of her legs, but they left little to the imagination. Coupled with the black heels and plunging neckline, she looked as if she were wearing the sort of maid costume they sold in Halloween stores, not something an actual human woman wore while serving cocktails at a posh party.

"Hey, I don't pick the uniforms," Gwen snorted, wiggling at me. "Hurry and zip me up. I'm *late*."

"So you keep saying," I muttered, rising and crossing the room. I zipped Gwen's back and tried tugging the dress up a little to cover even a millimeter more of her skin.

"It's no good. I already tried that," she muttered dryly, twisting in the bathroom mirror this way and that as she considered herself, patting down the puffed skirt.

I shook my head, crossing my arms. "Who exactly *is* responsible for this fetish wear?"

Gwen started laughing and adjusted the bow at the back of the apron. "Rumor has it that Tommie had these uniforms made specially, just for the occasion," Gwen said slyly, arching one brow at me. She picked up a tube of lipstick off the sink's rim and popped off the cap, then pursed her lips and carefully applied a smear of red. "But hey, as your straight best friend," she muttered as she winked at me, "I don't mind telling you that there's just as many guys as gals at this thing tonight, and I don't mind showing off a little skin. Everyone will probably tip great; I heard all the guests are *loaded.* And who knows? Maybe there'll be a super-loaded guy who will start this amazing conversation with me, be as turned on by my brain as my bod, and I could get lucky!"

I laughed and shook my head. "Just remember that I'm shacking up with you tonight," I quipped, as Gwen blotted her lips with a tissue. "If you *have* to bring a guy back to your room, give me some sort of warning so I can go for a walk or…something."

"I'd probably be going to *his* room, sugar," said Gwen with a wide, cheesy grin as she tossed the lipstick back onto the sink. "And, anyway, you know I'm all talk… I still haven't gotten over Gary."

I rolled my eyes so hard they were in danger of falling out. "That you ever *had* something with Gary to be *gotten over* is an incredible feat—"

"Hey, don't start in on that poor man again," Gwen sighed, smoothing down the front bodice and skimpy apron as she pouted in the mirror, pulling her hair up into a high bun and jabbing at the stray curls with bobby pins.

"I just think that you shouldn't mourn jerks," I said, then spread my hands as she glared at my reflection in the mirror. "And that's all I'll say on the matter."

"Yeah, well," Gwen muttered around a mouthful of bobby pins, "the past is behind us now, isn't it?"

My reflection took on a somber expression, and I turned, walking back into the bedroom as images of Anna filled my head.

If Melody had, in fact, talked to Kane about my leaving, if Kane really had agreed with her and wanted me to leave the Sullivan Hotel—for good—then that meant that I was headed back to Greensprings, New Hampshire…the town where Anna and I had started to build a life together before her accident. Before I'd lost her. Again, I'd be surrounded with a million reminders of the life we could have had together—and didn't. Again, I'd spend every day with a shadow from my past haunting my every moment. Again, I would spend every day mourning what could never be. Mourning her.

I…didn't want the rest of my days to be filled with regret.

Not about Anna.

And not about Kane.

And not about Tommie.

"Are you okay?" Gwen murmured, coming out of the bathroom. She looked ready to go, with her usually crazy mane of hair pinned up prettily, standing there in her ridiculous maid outfit.

"I'm all right," I told her with a soft smile. Which was the truth. The path my life took would never again be *chosen* for me. I would decide my own fate, I knew. I vowed.

Starting now. Vampires be damned.

"Have…fun?" I asked, and smiled again as I hugged her tightly.

"Wish me, like, a million dollars in tips," said Gwen, kissing me lightly on the cheek before heading quickly to her door.

"Good luck," I muttered, after she'd shut the door behind her.

For a long time after Gwen left, I thought about heading back to Tommie's rooms (not that she'd probably still be in them) and…finishing what we'd started. Whenever I considered the notion, my heart fluttered, and I fell into a reverie, remembering her cool lips pressed hard against mine...

True, I felt guilty for thinking about Tommie, but every time the guilt reared its ugly head, I reminded myself of the fact that Kane and I were not, and had never been, a couple.

Still, I was so confused. I'd think of Kane, and I'd close my eyes and feel, again, her arms, her mouth…that one cold, beautiful kiss…

I was driving myself crazy.

So instead of thinking about the two beautiful vampires that my mind and heart were obsessing over, I tried not to think at all.

I read some of the magazines Gwen had on her bedside table. They were mostly about yoga, and since I don't do yoga, all of the talk about asanas and proper posture went over my head. Eventually, I fell asleep with her bedside lamp on and a yoga magazine open beside me.

And I dreamed.

I stood on a tall balcony, many stories up from the ground, my fingers resting lightly on the elaborate bronze railing as I looked out to the sea. The sea breeze was so sharp, so cold, but I stood there, still and resolute despite the cold, my heart thundering in me.

I knew I was at the Sullivan Hotel, because behind me and below me was the familiar, tell-tale red stone of the building.

There were a dozen roses on the small, round table behind me, their crystal vase resting in the very center of the lace doily on the smooth and polished tabletop. They had just been brought to me by a small, shaky bellboy who probably wouldn't last long here, I thought. His subconscious knew he was surrounded by hunters, and even though they would never hunt him, he still feared them.

The roses were so fragrant, even on this windy, storm-tossed autumn day. The beautiful perfume reached my nose even here, even out on the balcony with the stiff salt breeze to cool me.

The roses unsettled me, but—in the dream—I couldn't remember exactly why. It was the feeling that I knew something, but couldn't quite remember it, and that sensation was maddening.

There was a knock at the door.

My heart began to beat faster, and I turned slowly, glancing down at myself. The dress I wore was so…big. With wide, large red skirts and something that squeezed me around my middle. I pressed my fingers to my unnaturally slimmed waist—a corset? The dress made moving slow, like I was treading through water, but I managed to stride off the balcony, through the room with its odd, antique decorations, to the door.

I opened it, and Tommie was there.

Like I knew she'd be.

She was wearing a men's suit, like she always does, but this one was a little different from her usual attire—more antique looking, with the waistcoat that bore a gold watch chain. Her hair was different, parted on the side and slicked back with grease, and her hat looked like something out of vaudeville. She had it in her hands in front of her, twisting the brim this way and that, and her mouth was in a downward turning grimace.

"You got the flowers," she said softly—not a question.

In the dream, I took a step back. There was something off, ominous between us as Tommie stepped into the room, as she shut the door softly behind us.

Like a confession was about to be made.

"I've done everything I could…" I stared at her in surprise as she choked down a sob, turning toward me, breathing out. Though she was cold, I knew, like all vampires, there was a heat that crackled between us. "Please believe me," she began, taking a deep breath to calm herself, searching my eyes with her own, flashing green ones, "that I have done everything I could to rid myself of you." She took one more step forward, and then she was standing right there before me, and her cold fingers were grasping my hand as tightly as any lifeline.

"I love you," she whispered, and my blood thundered through me as she fell to her knees brokenly, wrapping her arms tightly about my waist as she stared up at me, her face contorted in pain. "Tell me what you will, tell me that I must stop in this pursuit of you. But I can not. I feel for you something I have never felt, and *she*…" The word was spat out between us. "*She* has everything. She's always had everything. She has you, and I will never have a chance with you because of her. But you can change that. Give me one word of kindness, just one and—"

"Tommie, please…" I whispered, trying to take a step back as she gripped me tightly. It was not my voice that spoke those words—it was a voice I almost didn't recognize, but did enough to wonder where I'd heard it before. "You ask of me an impossibility," I murmured, my hands closing over hers behind me as I breathed out. "Please understand, I care about you. I care about you truly. You are a very good friend."

Tommie looked so betrayed, so utterly gutted, that my heart felt like it was breaking. "A friend," she whispered. Her hands fell away from me, and she rose slowly, her knees dusty as she stood, her fingers shaking. "And is that all I may ever hope for?"

I stood so still, felt the weight of the moment so deeply as I whispered: "my heart belongs to another."

"Kane," said Tommie slowly, evenly. She bit her lip, put her hat on her head and breathed out. "Of course. But I had to know. I had to try. I have loved you," she said, then, and when she looked up at me, the fervency in her eyes took my breath away. "And I won't stop," she murmured. "I can not."

The door closed behind her strongly, and an especially unfurled rose shuddered against its brothers in the crystal vase.

A single petal dislodged and plummeted to the note that had been pinned to the vase, that I'd taken from its pin and read and let drop to the tabletop because it was too painful to hold. How Tommie had repeated the words "I love you" over and over again in tiny, desperate pen strokes.

But as I strode forward to look down at the note, I couldn't quite see it, because a voice was calling my name…

Which is how Gwen woke me up.

"Oh, my God, Rose, I need your help," she hissed, shaking my shoulder again and again. Hard.

"What?" I mumbled, blinking my bleary eyes, trying to dislodge the ominous feeling the dream had given me. I rubbed at them and tried to focus on her. I hadn't taken off my makeup, and my mascara was making my eyelids glued together at the corners. "What's the matter?" I spluttered to her. "What time is it?"

"Almost eight. At night. Look, I'm so, so, *so* sorry to spring this on you," said Gwen, not even taking a breath as she bit her lip, tucking a loose curl behind her ear, "but you have *got* to help me—Rose, I'm desperate."

Immediately, I was sitting up in bed, searching for bite marks on Gwen's very exposed neck and shoulders. Nothing. Had she been bitten? Was she in trouble? My heart rate began to skyrocket. What could possibly have happened to her?

"What's the matter?" I asked, shoving hair out

of my eyes.

"It's Clare," said Gwen, all in a rush, her brows furrowed and stray curls of her hair escaping the pins. "She was supposed to help me serve the cocktails at this drawing room soiree or whatever the hell it is, but she *can't,* because she got sick. Something about bad chowder. She's *really* sick; she isn't faking. There's just no way she can help. And, oh, my God, there are so many *people*, Rose... Like a hundred or something in that one drawing room. I can't serve the cocktails alone, there's too many people. I've tried to manage, and I just can't—it's impossible. Please, please, please help me?"

My best friend clasped her hands and began to wring them in front of my eyes like a silent film actress in a very desperate situation.

"I'm going *mad*," Gwen continued after a second of my silence as I pieced everything together. "You don't even know. I mean, they want all of this special stuff, these really elaborate drinks that I don't have made up, because of course they're rich people, and rich people are picky, I guess. I don't know!" She was practically wailing as I opened my mouth and tried to say something, but she was shaking her head, continuing, "So then I have to rush down to the kitchens, and I'd like to point out that *we don't have an elevator,* and everyone wants something different, and if you don't help me, I think I'm going to keel over in ten more minutes. I can't do this alone," she moaned.

"You want me to help you serve cocktails," I managed, blinking. "But...I was fired—"

"Oh, who gives a shit about that? *I'll* pay you," said Gwen, her eyes wide.

"It's not about the money," I said quickly,

shaking my head. I would never take money from Gwen for helping her out. "It's Melody," I said softly, with a grimace. "If Melody sees me—"

"Let her. Everyone knows we're understaffed, and I challenge any *one* of those Sullivan women to argue against someone offering to help me in my hour of need," muttered Gwen, bristling. "If Melody says anything to you, *you just tell me.* It'll be like—justified homicide."

I smiled in spite of myself at my best friend's fierceness. The fact that Melody was a vampire—that if she didn't exactly like me being here, she could do something quite drastic and *final* about it—wasn't exactly a piece of information I could share with Gwen.

Honestly, though, I didn't think Melody would be so bold as to drain me dry.

Still, Mags had certainly tried it. I massaged my forehead and took a deep breath.

But the truth of the matter was this: I wasn't afraid of Melody. And I was no longer afraid of Mags. I didn't have anything to lose.

And that made me just as dangerous as they were.

"Okay," I said quickly, sliding my legs over the side of the bed and standing with a stretch. "Just tell me what to do and how to do it. I've never served cocktails before."

"You're a *lifesaver,*" Gwen said with a squeal, hugging me tightly. "There's just…one more thing," she murmured with a wince. She glanced down at herself.

And at her tiny, very revealing maid outfit.

"Oh, no," I muttered, holding up one hand. "I'll help you serve the cocktails, but I have to draw the line at a skirt that's too short to even be defined as a skirt."

"Hey, Tommie went to so much *trouble* to pick these costumes out." She held up another dry-cleaner's bag with a chuckle and a wink.

"Yeah, well, you can bet that I'm going to give Tommie an earful later," I muttered, snatching the bag from Gwen's hands and turning to trudge into the bathroom.

"You know she'd probably find that earful sexy," said Gwen from the bedroom, as I sighed with a smile and unzipped my skirt, unbuttoned my blouse and took off my clothes, stepping into the maid uniform.

One glance in the mirror, and I chuckled beneath my breath. Oh, God, I looked *completely* ridiculous.

I usually wear old-fashioned sorts of clothes. I guess my style is a little retro, classic, elegant, and when I wear costumes, I'm usually cross-dressing—as a pirate or a male vampire, laughably—not as a scantily clad female servant.

I looked genuinely pained and uncomfortable in the dress. I noticed as I turned in front of the mirror that I was trying to walk a little lower, with my knees bent—not that this would actually aid the skirt's ability to cover my rear.

I have a long torso and legs which requires me to wear long-waisted garments, or things just end up looking too short on me. It is a *very* specific woman who looks great in a *very* short skirt and plunging neckline.

And trust me: I was *not* that specific woman.

"Rose, I've already been gone ten minutes. We

might have a riot on our hands if we stay away any longer," Gwen muttered outside the door. I swept my hair up in a high ponytail and applied Gwen's lipstick, and then I was out the door, self-consciously shifting from one foot to the other as Gwen looked me up and down.

"Pretty terrible, right?" I asked, and Gwen wrinkled her nose, head to the side.

"I mean, no. It's not *bad*," she said carefully, which is Gwen's way of saying *yes, absolutely terrible* in the nicest way possible. "But we have to *go*," she said, threading her arm through mine and all but dragging me out her bedroom door and down the hallway.

Now that I was in the corridor where anyone could, in fact, *see* me in this ridiculous outfit, I felt more embarrassed than ever. A breeze could be felt in bodily regions that made me highly aware of how little I was wearing. We trotted down the spiral staircase to the drawing room floor, and we clicked across the red and black tiles as Gwen muttered information over her shoulder—how to hold the drinks tray; the fact that it was an open bar, so money wasn't changing hands, but that the guests were tipping.

If my run-in that morning with the hundred-dollar tipper was any indication, vampires tipped *very* well. So at least there was that to look forward to.

But it was a small consolation as we reached the drawing room door. The door was partially open, and a few vampires lingered outside of it, smoking and talking in small groups as they lounged against the wall. They didn't pay Gwen and me any sort of attention as we walked past them, and then we were in the drawing room itself, where it was, blessedly, dark enough that my hideous outfit would be partially hidden—I hoped.

The far wide fireplace was lit, and a few lamps were on, but their small bulbs were of such a low wattage that my eyes actually had to adjust from the dimly lit hallway to the *very* dimly lit drawing room.

The room was very crowded but hushed. Everyone spoke in low tones, and there were a few punctuations of laughter, but for the most part, vampires lounged on couches and chairs or leaned against walls and milled in the center of the room. It was a very low-key party, with cigarettes dangling from lips and wine glasses and martini glasses in hand as they bent their heads to one another and discussed things in soft voices.

"Here," Gwen whispered, picking up a tray of full glasses from a table by the door. "Carry it in front of you and ask people nicely if they'd like a drink. They'll put their finished glasses on your tray, too, if they have one, so bring those back to this table and keep going, okay?"

I nodded, took a deep breath and accepted the tray. I glanced around the room, steeling myself as I remembered who exactly was here. The tray itself and its glassware wasn't very heavy, but the prospect of interacting with Melody had taken the wind out of my sails. It's one thing to have bravado before the event, and another thing entirely to be brave *during* it. I was doing my best. I just didn't want a scene. I didn't want her to pick me apart in front of Kane, something I believed that she was entirely capable of doing.

I carried the antique tray into the room, aware of the wood against my palms, of the gentle clink of the glasses together as I shifted my weight to hold the tray more securely. The scent of tobacco, of expensive perfume and clove cigarettes began to merge with the scent of the alcohol as I drifted to the right, looking for a familiar face.

"Would you like a drink?" I asked the occupants of a low, red velvet loveseat, narrow but still long enough to hold five women. They'd had to get creative with the seating arrangements to make themselves all fit, however. Dolly sat on the far right end of the loveseat, in the lap of a woman dressed in a suit, the woman's buzz cut blonde hair and flashing eyes utterly captivating. Dolly herself was resplendent, her short blonde curls swept back from her face. She wore a plunging blue dress that the *Leave it to Beaver* mother might have shown off in a more liberated time than the fifties. Dolly leaned forward with a bright smile as she glanced up at me, her necklace of fat pearls dripping down over her décolletage and making her even more beautiful with its refined elegance. But, to be perfectly honest, Dolly would have been beautiful in a potato sack.

"Rose, are you helping Gwen out with the drinks? That's so wonderful of you! I heard about Clare being sick. That's just awful. I hope she's all right soon," said Dolly all in a rush as she snatched up a martini glass from my tray. "And, oh, my gosh, Rose, how lovely you look! You totally have the legs to pull off that dress. I don't think I could quite manage it," she laughed and winked at me.

"I think it's ridiculous," said Jane succinctly, from beside Dolly. She had her left ankle on her right knee and an arm around the woman who held Dolly in her lap. Jane's mouth was in a thin, hard line, and she looked as sour as usual as her eyes swept over me. She, too, wore a suit, her blonde hair formed into a pompadour style, the tie over her chest shot through with silver thread that glittered in the low light. She frowned deeper as she gave me the once over. "It's ludicrous, that maid's uniform. Why was Tommie permitted to be so self-indulgent?"

"No one else wanted to think about it, and Tommie stepped up to the plate," said Dolly. "And Rose looks *fine*, Jane. Don't be so insulting."

One of Jane's brows went up, and she shrugged, pointedly glancing elsewhere as she shot back the drink in her hands. It looked like a scotch.

"Does anyone else want a drink?" I asked the rest of the loveseat. My cheeks were flushed, but I doubted that anyone could make out my blush in the dark room.

When no one else took a glass or showed any interest in my question whatsoever, I left the loveseat and turned, carefully balancing the tray of drinks as a man brushed past me too closely, upsetting the balance of the tray on my hand. I steadied it, breathed out a sigh of relief, and glanced up.

And there was Kane.

My heart leapt into my throat as I stared at her, and she stared at me. She leaned, of course, against the fireplace—one of her favorite haunts in the room. And, of course, she held a slim cigarette to her lips. As I watched, she narrowed her eyes and inhaled deeply from it, the cigarette smoke spiraling up and around her face, shrouding her features for half a heartbeat…but incapable of shadowing her eyes. Even through the smoke, her powerful blue eyes burned their gaze into me, down into the very deepest parts of me.

I stood, stilled by an invisible force, as Kane and I gazed at one another.

Kane Sullivan, like always, held me spellbound.

Tearing my gaze away—because I had to; because I couldn't lose myself to those electrifying eyes again—I woodenly asked the next group of people if they'd like something to drink. I don't remember if anyone took a glass, or even if they acknowledged me. Because like a certain and absolute gravity, my entire body was turning toward Kane again. I was so close to the fireplace. A few more groups of vampires, asking them if they were thirsty (of course they were thirsty, but not for what I held in front of me) and a few more drinks taken, I'd be right in front of her, asking her that laughable question:

Can I get you anything? Are you thirsty?

Time moved forward too quickly. Because of course I went through those groups, asked my inane questions.

And then I was standing in front of her.

Kane flicked the ash off the end of her cigarette and regarded me with her head to the side, her mouth parted a little, her lips wet and glistening in the light from the fireplace. Or maybe she was wearing lip gloss—though she didn't really strike me as the type of woman to do such a thing. I stared at that mouth, couldn't help but stare at that exquisite mouth.

Kane shifted ever so slightly toward me, angling her body away from the crowds, leaning one shoulder against the mantle.

"How are you, Rose?" she asked with that beautiful, deep voice.

Considering the circumstances, considering what had happened to me today, I couldn't help but splutter, holding the tray tightly in front of me, like a shield.

"Maybe it isn't for the best," is what I managed

to tell her, then. Her brows furrowed, and those deep blue eyes narrowed further. I wanted to tell her that I didn't want to go. I wanted to tell her that I felt complete here, at the Sullivan Hotel.

I knew, in that moment, that even just seeing Kane every day would be enough for me. I knew, essentially, that that wasn't really true. Being tortured every day by the realization that someone I utterly and truly despised could hold and touch and kiss the woman who'd stolen my heart…I mean, it was the most masochistic way to live imaginable.

But I'd do it. I'd do it for her. To see her. To be near her.

My jaw clenched, and I worked up the courage to tell her this, because her face belied pain, beneath the surface of her skin, deep in her heart, as she leaned forward, toward me, so much taller than me. I inhaled the scent of her, and my knees—already weak—weakened further, and then her cold, sure fingers were at the curve of my hip, radiating coolness through the cloth of my tiny dress…

And Melody came sweeping out of the crowd, like a shark descending toward its prey with grim and absolute resolve. She snaked an arm around Kane's waist, and then she was glaring at me, her eyes flashing so dangerously, I took an involuntary step backward.

And Kane's touch left me.

I almost cried out from how painful that was, how my heart twisted inside of me, beating too quickly, searing and anguished.

"You have drinks to serve," Melody hissed at me, and then she wrapped her arms tightly around Kane's waist. But Kane didn't turn to meet Melody's body. She stood square, her feet hip-width apart, her jaw clenched, too, and her shoulders rigid as she watched me back away, back away from the both of them.

Kane opened her mouth to say something, her blue eyes bright, but she closed her mouth again after a heartbeat.

What could she say, after all?

Melody looked surprised that Kane wasn't turning toward her, wasn't responding to her obvious advances and signs of affection, but the surprise didn't last long. She stood up on her tiptoes and pressed her full lips to Kane's cheek. And then she began to whisper in Kane's ear.

It made me sick to my stomach to see how familiar she was with Kane. I turned, blinded by tears I *absolutely refused* to shed, and then I stood for a long moment, my back to the two of them, until I could turn and realize that the crowd had swallowed them from my view.

Why did it have to be so painful, seeing Melody with Kane?

Why did it have to feel *so wrong*? A kind of wrongness that made my insides cry out, that made my heart stir in me. There was so much injustice in the entire arrangement, and at that moment, I couldn't have told you why I felt like that.

I just knew that Kane and Melody together was…wrong.

I moved on to a low antique sofa and woodenly opened my mouth to inquire whether the occupants of it were thirsty, my heart aching so dangerously it was hard to draw a deep breath.

Branna lounged on that couch, her legs crossed, and her men's suit being worn with such grace that no one could ever call it a "man's" suit again—it was solely meant for her. Her red-brown hair was perfectly greased back, and she was tugging a little at her bow tie to loosen it around her neck when she glanced up at me, and her large brown eyes widened as she took me in.

She stood in one smooth motion, and put a gentle hand at my back. "Are you all right?" she asked me quietly, steering me toward the door and the table to set my tray of drinks on.

"I'm fine," I told her, just as quietly. We could both hear the lie in my voice.

"Rose, what's going on?" asked Branna, when I finally set the tray on the table. She took my shoulders in her hands and held me steady, staring down and into my eyes, her brow furrowed. "Is it Melody?"

"*Yes,* it's Melody…" I didn't know exactly what to tell her. Her kind, gentle gaze and her concern were making my stomach knot and all of the tears I'd been choking down were now threatening to spill. "You were really wonderful to me, Bran," I told her, then, gazing up at her and—stepping forward—embracing her tightly.

The vampire froze under my show of affection, and I stepped back, suddenly self-conscious. "I'm sorry," I managed, wiping my eyes with the back of my hand. I drew in a deep breath. "I'm going to miss you," I told her then, my voice small.

Her eyes grew wider. "What are you talking about? You're leaving?"

I shook my head. "Didn't you hear? I thought everyone would have heard by now," I added a little bitterly. I spread my hands. "Melody fired me. I'm going to try to talk to Kane about it, beg my case…I don't really want to leave the Sullivan Hotel. Even after…everything." I waved my hand in the direction of the fireplace, of Melody and Kane who I couldn't see, but I knew were there, Melody's arms possessively around Kane. Sometimes, the way that Melody clung to Kane felt like they were out at sea, and Melody was determined to pull Kane under the water forever.

Branna's wide, brown eyes changed, then. I'd never seen her gaze harden, but it did now as she straightened, as her jaw hardened, too. She softened a little as she looked down at me. "Don't worry," she said gently, reaching out and squeezing my hand with her own cold fingers. "It's going to be fixed," she promised, her voice soothing.

She turned and quickly disappeared in the crowd.

But I didn't want Branna to fight my battles for me, as sweet as that was. I began to stride after her, but I wasn't exactly looking where I was going, in the dark room, and my thigh connected with the arm of a sofa.

And then I stopped in my tracks.

There was Tommie. She'd changed her clothes, was still wearing dress pants, but now there was a suit jacket over her white dress shirt, and a different tie. The fedora was pulled down low over her face, and she was chatting up a blonde vampire who was so pretty that I couldn't believe she was real. The blonde's hair, formed in scalloped waves down her back, practically glowed, and her dress looked like it'd been sewn onto her body, a soft, shiny black satin that hugged her tightly, delivering the perfect hourglass shape, like she was an ultra curvy silhouette of the perfect woman. I couldn't exactly tell if the dress's color was black or a very dark shade of purple—not that the color actually mattered. Her red lips were close to Tommie's cheek as she whispered something into her ear, making Tommie chuckle softly.

Tommie's hand was on the vampire's thigh, her fingers resting lightly under the woman's knee-length skirt.

Tommie glanced up, and to her credit, she paled upon seeing me. She leaned back on the couch, slowly removing her hand from the vampire's leg.

"Rose? What are you doing here?" she asked mildly.

"Helping Gwen," I managed, clearing my throat. I gestured back toward the table at the room's entrance with a grimace and tried to sound sincere—but it came out a little sarcastically: "Would you like a drink?" The blonde vampire's eyebrows were raised, and she wasn't looking at me but smirking and glancing sidelong at Tommie.

"No, thank you," said Tommie softly. Then she was standing, tugging at her suit jacket's lapels as she cleared her throat.

I didn't say anything. I turned on my heel, my cheeks burning, to continue along the wall to follow Bran.

"Rose, wait," said Tommie tiredly, and then she was right behind me, her sure fingers tight around my elbow again. But it was the same hand that had been resting against that woman's thigh, and I shrugged out of her grasp, stepping sideways.

"I'm sorry. I have work to do," I said woodenly, trying to glimpse Branna in the crowd—but she'd completely disappeared from view.

I wasn't really certain what to feel. I felt a little ill from the night's events, to be honest. Kane. Then

Melody. And now this.

I wasn't stupid. I knew that Tommie hadn't promised me *anything* with that kiss. It was, after all, just a kiss.

But I guess I'd been hoping… Well, I don't really know what I'd been hoping for. After all, this was just who Tommie was. I shouldn't have expected anything else. I don't know why I did.

"Can't you talk for a moment?" sighed Tommie in exasperation. "Look—"

"I have to help Gwen," I told Tommie crisply. It was, after all, the only reason I was subjecting myself to this terrible night, to help out my best friend who deserved more than me standing around and talking to vampires. I needed to start serving the drinks again...

Then Tommie spread her hands and shrugged, taking a step back. She was swallowed up by the milling crowd, and I breathed out for a long moment before heading back to the room's entrance. I moved quickly back to the door to the drawing room, but there were no more trays there with drinks, only empty ones. Gwen was halfway into the room with a full tray upon her hands, a wide smile on her face as she asked a small group of male vampires if they'd like a drink. They were all pointedly staring at her very bare neck, which caused me to shiver. But they wouldn't do anything—not here.

And hell—maybe they'd tip her even better.

A few days into the Sullivan Hotel and I was getting *cynical* about vampires. I sighed for a long moment and picked up an empty tray.

Gwen said that she'd kept going back down to the kitchens, so maybe that's where I could go to refill these trays. Several floors down. I sighed but stacked the trays together and put them under my arm, placing the glasses in a large plastic wash bin under the table that was starting to become full with dirty stemware. I glanced back once into the room, but the space was too crowded; I couldn't see Bran.

I couldn't see Kane.

And I could find Tommie. And that, I realized, was probably for the best.

Tommie could do what she wanted with herself. She owed no loyalty to me.

But the sight of her hand on the woman's leg had still stung.

Just like the sight of Melody's arm around Kane's waist.

I couldn't do anything about either of them. They were their own women.

But my heart still twisted inside of me as I pushed my way out of the drawing room and into the corridor. The lights were so bright—in comparison to those in the drawing room—that it took a moment for my gaze to adjust. I set off down the now empty corridor with the trays, heading toward the spiral staircase.

And I turned a corner.

And there was Tommie.

She was leaning against the wall nonchalantly, like a detective in a noir film, her hands deep in her pockets, her dress shirt unbuttoned at the top, an unlit cigarette dangling from her lips. I'd found out that most of the Sullivan women smoked, but none nearly as much as Kane. Tommie hardly ever lit up but often had a pack of cigarettes on her "just in case." A very long life had its advantages, I supposed.

I paused, biting my lip as Tommie pushed off

from the wall, plucking up her cigarette and neatly threading it through her fedora's hatband. She cocked her head at me with a frown.

"We've got to stop meeting like this," I said after a long moment. I'd meant to be funny, but the words came out half-choked, and I swallowed, holding the trays tighter to me.

"I'm sorry," she said gruffly, then, forming the words slowly, as if she wasn't used to uttering them. "I thought you were leaving the hotel. It was…upsetting to me. That woman—she doesn't mean anything. I'm really sorry, Rose."

I was astonished.

Again, this inscrutable, sarcastic woman was baring her heart to me, casting her vulnerability at my feet.

She didn't have to apologize.

But she did, anyway.

"It's none of my business what you do—you don't owe me anything," I told her, but the words were gentle, and I felt my shoulders subtly relax.

Tommie stepped forward, her bright green gaze burning into my eyes. "Rose," she said, and the word was sad and small…desperate. "I *want* it to be your business," she said softly.

And then, just like that, she was kissing me again.

She'd threaded her fingers into the hair at the base of my neck, pulled back loosely with the ponytail. It felt so good, her cool fingertips against my scalp, the length of her hard body pressed against mine. It felt so good, how she cradled my face with her palms, first gently, and then her hands were moving down, over my bare shoulders, making me shiver, before clasping my waist tightly. Her mouth against me tasted of nicotine and scotch; her lips were warm and soft and dangerous and desperate as she kissed me hard, holding me hard.

I pressed against her, too. I'd been desperately jealous of that blonde woman, of the casual way Tommie's fingers had worked under the hem of her skirt. They'd just rested against that woman's knee, it was true, but I hadn't wanted Tommie to touch her.

I'd wanted Tommie to touch *me*.

I realized, then, as Tommie's mouth devoured mine, as her lips began to make a hot, wet trail to the lobe of my ear, down my neck, as I shivered against her, that I wanted this very much.

Everything else faded away when Tommie touched me, when she kissed me. There was no outside world. There was no Kane, who made my heart ache, no Melody, who made me so very angry. No injustice. No loss. There was nothing but the two of us together, anchored to one another with mouths and hands, bodies pressed against one another like we were all that held the other up.

Tommie made me forget my pain, made me forget all of the things I'd wanted so much that I could never have now.

Tommie made me forget Kane.

Tommie's mouth was on mine again, and my arms were wrapped around her neck, the trays against her back as I tried to hold onto them with only my fingers, as Tommie's hands still held my hips tightly, the fluff of my skirts flattened between us.

I hardly noticed the cool click of shoes sounding out hollowly in the corridor behind me, from the direction of the drawing room. But when Tommie glanced up, her eyes dark with desire, a savage anger passed over her face.

And then I turned and went cold—body and soul.

It was Kane.

She strode toward us slowly, with measured steps, one hand gracefully holding a cigarette that she took an occasional pull from. Out in the better light of the corridor, it was easy to appreciate her outfit, with the red shirt and the plunging neckline and the high-collared jacket. Her bright blue eyes were narrowed, too, as she took in the scene before her.

She flicked the ash off the end of her cigarette, which dangled from the tips of her fingers as she sighed out for a long moment, clearing her throat.

"Rose, Tommie," she said, her low, gravelly voice sending a shiver down my spine. Tommie frowned, tightening her hands at my hips.

Maybe I was reading too much into it, but Tommie seemed to be conveying, with her forward posture, with the way that she'd widened her stance on the floor, her feet now hip-width apart as she leaned towards Kane with a hard frown, that she was saying, very clearly, "Mine."

I glanced from Tommie to Kane, feeling my heart break into two very sharp pieces. Kane took another pull from her cigarette as she gazed into my eyes. Hers were hard slits, but as I gazed deeper, I saw that hardness give away to pain as she shook her head, dropping the cigarette and stomping down on it slowly with the toe of her shoe.

It made a light scratching sound against the marble, and then there was only the distant hum of murmuring voices and laughter.

The corridor itself was as silent as the grave.

"I'm sorry for whatever happened earlier. With Melody," said Kane, her voice so low, it was almost a growl. "I want you to know that you don't have to leave the Sullivan Hotel, Rose. Not unless you choose to. Your position here is safe for however long you want it." It sounded so official as she squared her shoulders, as she lifted her head, not looking directly at us as she turned a little, putting her hands into her pockets, glancing sidelong at me with deep blue eyes that pinned me to the spot. "It seems," she murmured softly, "that there are others who want you here as much as I do."

"*More*, Kane," said Tommie, her teeth gritting together as her fingers tightened so strongly on my hips they were almost painful. I breathed out as Tommie's eyes darkened. "*Much* more than you do."

Kane exhaled. She stood very still for such a long moment, I could actually feel my heart aching within me.

She turned, then, her face in profile carefully controlled, carefully neutral, and she walked away slowly, the corridor shadowing her long, lank form until she'd reached the drawing room again, pulling the great door open and closing it quietly behind her.

Tommie's mouth found my neck, and she brushed her cold lips against my skin there as my heart thundered in me, as I realized what exactly had just transpired.

Some things had changed irrevocably:

I could stay.

Tommie wanted me.

And Kane did not.

# -- Eternal Heartbreak --

I woke up in a bed I didn't recognize, an arm wrapped loosely around my waist, and a body pressed tightly to my back.

This, normally, wouldn't be a bad way for most people to wake up. But as my heart rate accelerated, as I breathed out and in, my pulse quickening through my body, I felt a sense of dread come over me.

I didn't remember falling asleep.

I *certainly* didn't remember falling asleep next to someone. I glanced up at the ceiling, cast a cursory glance around the room.

I was in someone else's bed and someone else's room.

Yes, I knew I'd had a bit to drink last night. I remembered that much, at least. But I couldn't remember much else yet, as the waves of hangover started to wash over me with slow but insistent chills. I stared down at what I could see of the arm wrapped tightly around my waist. The soft, flowing curve of her skin was a welcome, lovely sight…but I didn't recognize that arm. Her limb was cold against my stomach—I was wearing a shirt, but it had ridden up slightly in sleep, which meant her skin pressed against mine. I shivered a little as I took a deep breath, realizing how cold the body was against my back. She was curved against me tightly, spooning me like this was the most natural thing in the world. Not the most unexpected.

A voice made a small murmur in her sleep, the tone a low, pleasant growl, and there was finally some spark of recognition. I took a deep breath.

I recognized that voice. I remembered.

I was in bed with Tommie.

I rolled over a little onto my side and turned to look at her over my shoulder. Tommie Sullivan was, thankfully, still fast asleep as my head spun and I tried, desperately, to make sense of what might have happened to me last night. Tommie was wearing a white tank top that showed off her sculpted, muscular shoulders, drawing my eyes down her lithe, long frame. I bit my lip as I breathed out softly, taking in the closeness of her, the sharp, chill scent of her skin and the lingering sweet smoke of the cigars she liked. My eyes traveled her length, even as my mind tried to grapple with why I was here. I tried, desperately, to remember.

In sleep, Tommie didn't look nearly as hard as she was when awake, with her sarcastic, sideways smile, and her eyes narrowed as she delivered scathing one-liners. Here, asleep, her face was softer, her long lashes resting gently against her cold, pale cheekbones. Those lashes fluttered just then, as if she was having a dream. Her soft lips were parted, her breath coming in a low, easy rhythm, breath that carried that sweet, lingering tobacco.

My blood was starting to pound even quicker through me. Frankly, Tommie looked gorgeous lying there. Gorgeous and…disheveled. Her short, shiny, raven-black hair lay tousled around her face. Maybe she tossed and turned a lot during the night.

Or maybe we'd slept together?

Blood rushed to my cheeks as I considered that possibility. God, I honestly couldn't *remember,* and that was *crazy*. Why the hell couldn't I remember if I'd *slept* with this gorgeous creature? Okay. I took a deep breath, wracked my brains while my pulse roared through me and I tried desperately to remember absolutely everything I could about the previous evening.

There had been the cocktail party last night—complete with me wearing that ridiculous maid outfit that Tommie had commissioned for the servers to wear. The poufy, frilly, too-short-for-anyone dress was now hanging off the edge of the foot bedpost. I plucked at the thin fabric covering my chest. I must have been wearing one of Tommie's tank tops, because it certainly wasn't mine. I tugged it down a little over my panties as I stared over my shoulder at Tommie again with a small grimace. I was, of course, not wearing pajama bottoms. Just panties. But I was still *wearing* panties… *Think*, Rose!

I remembered Kane telling me I should stay at the Sullivan Hotel.

With cold dread, I remembered Kane's indifference as she'd turned away from me. Of her piercing blues eyes that pinned me to the spot when she found me and Tommie together, Tommie's arms wrapping around me as she leaned closer, as our mouths met. Kane had found Tommie and me locked in an embrace…and kissing.

I sighed and ran a hand through my long, tangled red hair as I pieced the previous night together, dread beginning to grow in me. There was no specific reason for that dread. After all, I could stay at the Sullivan Hotel now, Melody be damned. She couldn't tell me to leave because Kane had overruled her, and Kane—as owner of the Sullivan Hotel—certainly had the last word. So this meant at least—for the time being—my job was secured.

But the dread grew in me as I remembered Kane's grave face in profile, turning away from Tommie and me, Tommie who was possessively gripping my hips with her long, cold fingers, her mouth at my neck.

Did I sleep with Tommie last night?

*Okay, get a grip*, I thought to myself, willing my heartbeat to slow down, and concentrating on making my breathing more regular. I'd only been terribly, painfully, *absurdly* drunk about three or four times in my life (I'd been pretty boring in college—I wasn't the party girl type—and then I'd gotten together with Anna, who'd never been much of a drinker herself), and each of those times, I'd still been able to remember what I'd been up to that previous night. Certainly, I'd wake up the next morning with the most killer headache imaginable, and a stomach that wanted me dead, but at least I'd *remember what had happened to me.*

I took a deep breath, calming my racing heart and the panic that was rising in me. The anxiety shed off of me like petals as I took some long, deep, cleansing breaths and as my head slowly began to clear, as I began to relax, it was then—of course—that I remembered.

I remembered Tommie walking me back to her room, my arm around her shoulder, because after the party had died down and I'd taken the drink trays back down to the kitchen, I'd helped myself to the remaining wine in the bottles. Gwen had told me that the Sullivans didn't mind, that they encouraged their employees to partake of everything that was left over from their meetings, get togethers or parties. And that included partaking of as much of the leftover booze that I could stomach. And because I'd been upset about the situation with Kane and Tommie and Melody, and what I'd been through that day…I'd had my fair share of that wine.

The problem with all of that is that I'm really not the best at *holding* wine. So after a couple of deep glasses last night, I'd gotten tipsy and then drunk…terribly drunk, really, as I'd kept playing that look of disappointment on Kane's face over and over again in my mind's eye, and kept pouring myself another glass, even after Gwen told me I should probably stop.

It was a terrible idea, admittedly, to drink when I was that upset, but I'd been *too* upset to think clearly, and the wine was there, ready to make things just a little softer…and then Tommie had been there, too, appearing out of nowhere in her suit jacket and her sarcastic, gorgeous smile. And Tommie had helped me to her room. I think the reason was that the locks were still changed on my door, so, technically, I really didn't have anyplace else to go, and Tommie had wanted to make certain I had someplace.

Or, perhaps, Tommie had just wanted to take me back to her room—and, in all honesty, I had been more than willing to go. So we went.

Tommie had also helped me out of my absurd maid's outfit, apologizing and chuckling in turns at my outrage over it. She'd gently pulled me into one of her old tank tops because I was so sore from serving drinks and carrying the heavy drink trays all night that I could hardly get my hands over my head (and, admittedly, too drunk to find the arm holes in the tank top). I don't remember Tommie's fingers lingering on my skin—it had been done discretely and kindly, her helping me out of that dress and into a shirt, even though I'd been naked in front of her, practically, even though I'd tripped as I'd stepped out of the dress and fallen against her. She'd helped me upright, her eyes averted, her cold hands at my waist. I remember that much. And then Tommie had eased me into bed and curled up behind me, her body tightly against mine, her arm still around my waist like she was never letting go.

As I lay in Tommie's bed that morning, Tommie still holding me tightly, I stared up at the barren white ceiling of her bedroom and let out a deep breath that I hadn't even realized I'd been holding. Now, with a clear head that I hadn't done anything stupid while I was drunk, I considered things.

If I slept with Tommie Sullivan, I wanted it to *mean* something. I didn't want it to be some stupid one-night stand, or a drunken, fumbling endeavor that was purely meaningless. I wanted it to be real, to have build up and emotions and...I wanted a relationship with anyone I slept with. I hadn't been with anyone since Anna. I wasn't about to start meaningless sexual dalliances.

But maybe (just maybe), I was actually ready to start another relationship.

I took a deep breath as Kane's face flashed in my mind's eye again, her piercing blue eyes staring clearly into mine, her chin up and her mouth in a thin, hard line. But I shouldn't think about Kane anymore, I reminded myself (somewhat painfully). After all, Kane had made it very clear last night that she didn't want me. And, anyway, she had Melody back now, her soul mate. She wasn't alone. She had the woman she'd wanted more than anything else on Earth.

There was absolutely nothing holding me to Kane anymore, if there had *ever* been anything to hold me to her.

I watched Tommie breathing slowly, her soft lips parted as she inhaled and exhaled with a sensual, constant rhythm. Everything Tommie did was sensual, from the act of taking off her hat to rake her fingers through her hair or when she leaned against the wall, hands shoved deeply into her pockets as she brooded moodily over something. She practically exuded raw sensuality, grace, ease…she was magnetic, and it was fairly obvious (at least, I was pretty certain) that with that much charm, Tommie had been with a *lot* of other women. Coming from that, I wasn't certain about what Tommie necessarily wanted with *me*.

But as I watched her sleep, I thought about what *I* wanted with Tommie. I bit my lip as my gaze trailed down her cheek and chin and neck to the low cut of her tank top and the small rise of her breasts.

Beside me, Tommie made a little grumbling sound in the back of her throat again as her eyelashes fluttered, and then she opened her eyes, blinking slowly as her gaze focused on me. And in a single instant, a sardonic smile began to curl her lips up at the corners, a smile that sent a shiver through me. "Good morning," she growled to me, and then she slowly leaned forward, the bed creaking gently beneath her shifting body, as she pressed her cold mouth to my bare shoulder.

A shudder raced through me, and my heart started beating quickly all over again. Her lips were very cold against my skin, but it was a delicious kind of cold, a kind of cold I craved. Her fingertips moved slowly, but with a determined patience, up and under the hem of my tank top.

My body responded quicker than my heart did. I turned over completely, lying on my back as I stared up at her, my heart pounding at a faster rate than my blood could take.

All I knew, in that moment, was need. And I knew, in that moment, that if I responded to that need, I would be making a mistake.

I was still too upset from last night. I was hung over. This wasn't how I wanted my first time with Tommie to be.

I bit my lip and her fingers paused. She stared down at me, and I realized that her breath was coming faster, her pupils were darker.

She felt it, too.

"I just…I need a little time," I managed to tell her. "I…I really like you, Tommie," I said quietly, as her dark eyes pinned me in place for a moment, as she held my gaze fiercely. "But so much has happened in the past few days…I don't know if I'm coming or going." I licked my lips, felt my own disappointment fill me. But, seriously, I didn't want it to be like this. I wanted to be able to brush my teeth and take a really great shower and smell better than spilled wine and I wanted it to be *sexy*, not self-conscious…

Because I knew that I *did* want this. I wanted Tommie.

Kane wasn't mine, and she never would be. And I had to start being all right with that fact.

"Give me a little time?" I whispered, holding her gaze.

For a long moment, I honestly didn't know what she'd say. But then a slow smile began to turn up the corners of her mouth again, and she nodded, raising one eyebrow as she lay back down on the bed beside me. "Of course," she said, her voice a low growl. But she kept her fingers beneath the hem of the tank top. "I want to try this with you, Rose," she said then, and the joking glint in her eyes was gone, the truth of her as clear as day and visible, flashing in her eyes. There was so much raw sincerity there. "Take the time you need," she told me.

I wanted to roll over and go up on my elbows over her, run my fingers through her hair, bring my mouth to hers. Everything about Tommie was easy like that. I fiercely held on to her gaze and tried not to think about Kane's sad expression in profile, tried not to think about Kane at all. It was hard.

Kane's shadow was cast over the possibility of Tommie and me. But we could still make it work, even though I still had feelings for Kane.

Right?

Tommie's fingers slipped out from beneath my shirt, and she traced a line up over the fabric to my face, curling her cool fingers around my chin and drawing me to her. Her mouth met mine, and for a long, searing moment, I thought about absolutely nothing at all. Instead, I *felt* everything.

When we broke apart, Tommie held my gaze for a long moment before she raised a single brow and slid effortlessly out from under the sheet and stood at the side of the bed, stretching overhead slowly. She was wearing a white tank top and black panties, and I couldn't help but stare at her muscled back, at the curve down to her rear.

"Do you…work out?" I asked, realizing even as I said it that it's one of the worst pick up lines *ever*. She turned to me actually chuckling, and there was nothing hard about her expression—she was genuinely amused by what I'd just asked.

"I'm a *vampire*," she said, placing a hand on one hip that she then jutted out, curving toward me so that I could feel a blush rising in my cheeks. Her panties were boy briefs, and I was doing my best not to stare at them. "Vampires don't work out," she said then, chuckling with a smooth shrug. "We retain the body that we had when we became a vampire," she raised her eyebrows and ran a hand down her arm, over the muscles there. "I worked in the stables when I was bitten, so I was pretty fit." She leaned forward a little, pressing her hands to the mattress as she bent at the waist, her face close to mine. "I dressed like a boy," she said then with a sexy smirk. "So I was given men's work to do. And I did it."

I realized as I stared up at her at that moment that I didn't really know anything about Tommie. I knew she was funny and sarcastic and gorgeous, that we were drawn to each other…but I wanted to get to know this enigmatic, charming woman. I wanted to know everything about her.

I was realizing that for some strange reason…there was something very familiar about Tommie. Though I'd never met her in my life, it felt like I knew her. Or *had* known her. It was such a strange feeling that I pushed it away, running a hand through my hair absent-mindedly. I had enough to worry about without thinking something that absurd. It was obvious that there was no way that I could have ever met Tommie before. I put the thought out of my mind.

"I'm on the schedule for today," I told her,

rolling up and out of the bed, feeling my blush intensify as her eyes made no secret about drifting down over my hardly-clothed body. "Anyway," I muttered, clearing my throat, "I'm supposed to cover the front desk until Gwen takes over at five…" I trailed off, bit my lip, screwed up my courage. "Do you want to do something after that?" I asked, clearing my throat again. I coughed a little into my hand and tried to stand not awkwardly. It had been a *really* long time since a woman had seen this much of me. My breasts were almost completely visible in this practically see-through tank top, and I was only wearing panties below. It was different for Tommie, who wore much the same clothes. I didn't feel confidant, like her, as I stood there, as that gorgeous vampire's eyes were roving over my body like she was memorizing me.

Tommie leaned back on her heels and shrugged elegantly. "Do you like boats?" she asked me then with a wolfish grin.

"I like boats," I replied, feeling the corners of my mouth turn up. Tommie's smiles were completely infectious.

"Well, I have a nice boat," she said, her smirk deepening. She softened, then, too as she inclined her head toward me. "I'd like to show you my boat tonight. After the sun sets. Maybe I could take you out, get some stargazing under our belts? Possibly something else under your belt," she said so softly that I wondered if I'd even heard her right, but then she was moving impossibly fast, and she was standing right there in front of me.

And she was hooking her fingers into the band of my panties.

She just hooked them there, like you hook

fingers into belt loops. She was pressed against the front of me, her chill body making my arms break out into goose flesh, even as another shiver raced through me.

"That…that sounds like it'd be wonderful," I told her, and I reached my hands up and wrapped my fingers around her waist. I felt her muscles beneath my palms, and something akin to hunger went through me.

"Good. Six o'clock," she said quietly, winking at me before stepping back. "Let's meet out front?"

"Sure," I said, and I knew that my voice had squeaked when I'd said it, but I managed to run a frazzled hand through my hair and take a deep breath. I smiled tentatively at her.

This was all so new to me. I had to carefully not think about Kane, and then things were sort of all right. If I didn't think about anything, actually, all of my feelings could just kick in. Yes. I wouldn't think about things.

"You'll have to speak to Kane about getting your lock changed back," said Tommie quietly then.

And all of my thoughts became, inevitably, about Kane.

"Sure," I said, biting my lip as I turned away from her, picking up my maid's outfit from the foot of the bed. I didn't want Tommie to see how even the mere *mention* of Kane's name affected me. I plucked at the hem of the too-short dress as I shifted it from one arm to the other. "Um…" I realized, glancing down at the thing and very forcefully pushing all thoughts of Kane from my mind. "I have to go get dressed, get ready for work," I told her, holding up the flimsy dress from last night. "I'll head to Gwen's room, but I can't exactly walk up the stairs or the hallways dressed like…um…" I waved down to myself and the tank tops and panties and made a grimace.

"Why not?" asked Tommie, leaning back against her bedpost with another wicked grin.

I raised a single eyebrow as I smiled at her, shaking my head.

"All right, all right," she muttered with a low chuckle. "You can borrow whatever you want," she told me, indicating her large, antique wardrobe with a sweep of her arm. "Anyway," she told me, glancing at the stark clock on the opposite side of the room. Both plain hands of the clock were pointing to seven. "I've got to get going," she said with a soft sigh. "We're having a…well, I suppose a meeting," she said, raising her brow as she peeled her tank top up and over her shoulders with absolutely no ceremony.

I blushed scarlet and stared down at the wooden floor, but not before I'd seen her in her entirety.

Her breasts were small, her nipples dark, and every curve of her was perfect.

I felt the floor fall out beneath me, because a war had just broken out inside of me. I'd been trying to ignore it and deny it, but it broke out all the same.

My feelings for Kane were violently and bitterly in battle with my feelings for Tommie.

Both women were so utterly different. How I'd felt for Anna was nothing like how I felt about Kane, and what I felt for Kane was absolutely nothing of how I felt for Tommie. I had affectionately and fiercely loved Anna. And, with Kane, there was a bone-deep knowledge that there was something between us.

But, strangely enough, I felt that there was something between Tommie and I, too. It was just…different.

I realized, in that moment, that I was feeling very, very confused. I needed to figure out what was happening inside of me, try to sort out these millions of strong feelings and figure out what I really wanted. I needed time alone to myself, to think.

But I wasn't going to get that. I had to work.

"Thank you," I told Tommie, then, taking a deep gulp of air as I realized that I hadn't yet thanked her for her offer to let me borrow anything in her wardrobe. I pulled the wide wardrobe doors open and began rummaging through her immaculately hung clothes. Each piece of clothing resided on a separate wooden hanger, and it was as neat as a pin inside of the wardrobe, everything hung in one orderly line.

Unsurprisingly, there were only suits lining the walls of the wardrobe. Tommie came up behind me, still completely naked on top and only wearing her boy short panties, and pulled the drawer open at the bottom of the wardrobe.

"I have other things in here," she said, crouching down beside me. I hazarded a glance at her, at the sculpted shoulders and narrowing in at her waist that was, at once, so strong and yet so feminine. She was still her powerful self, even without a shirt, but there was also a trace of the vulnerability that she showed when she slept. I liked that. I liked to know that there was something soft about her, that she wasn't all aggression and sarcasm all the time. That she could even be softer.

Tommie pulled something blue out of the bottom drawer and stood, holding it out to me. I stared at it in shock.

It was actually a dress.

There was not a single moment where I assumed that Tommie had ever worn this, or that it actually belonged to her. "How do you have this?" I asked her, taking the garment and being careful to stare at it and not at her. It was a very pretty dress, perhaps the kind that someone might wear to the office, complete with a black belt that I hadn't seen at first that dangled from the loops at the sides.

"Well…" she said, and trailed off, grabbing a shirt off one of the hangers and tossing it over her shoulders, sliding her arms in and beginning to button herself up at the lowest button. She was taking it slowly, I realized, as she stared at me unblinkingly with flashing eyes. "Someone…left it," she said softly then, the words barely audible. Then she straightened her shoulders, finished buttoning the shirt up to her neck. "I want to be up front with you about things. This time…" she said, leaning forward and taking my hands in her own cold fingers and drawing them up to clasp them tightly to her heart. "This time is different," she said the words firmly as she stared into my gaze, pinning me to the spot with a dazzling intensity.

Her body was so cold, even beneath the fabric of her shirt, and I could feel my heart pounding through me as my fingers caressed her breast as she cupped my hands in her own, holding them to her chest. She leaned down then, brushing her cold mouth over the backs of my knuckles before she released my hands.

The dress had fallen to the floor between us, and I crouched down with unseeing eyes, scooping it back up. I pulled it on over my head, over her tank top, and it fell around me, the edge of the tank top just visible at the neckline of the dress.

"Beautiful," she whispered, stepping forward and brushing her cold lips against my cheek before she walked away, sliding her arms into a suit jacket.

I glanced down at the fabric of the dress's skirt, touching that fabric with suddenly cold fingers.

The blue of the dress was the exact same blue as Kane's eyes.

"Thank you," I whispered to Tommie, tucking a strand of my hair behind my ear as I moved into her bathroom. I shut the door behind me, gripping the edge of the ornate sink and staring at myself in the mirror.

My reflection stared back at me with wide eyes. I looked confused.

Because I was.

That night, after a very long, boring time behind the front desk (most of the vampires who were attending the Conference had already checked in, so I was basically manning the desk in case anyone came down to ask a question or needed something. And it's not like vampires need extra washcloths and toothbrushes for their room. At least, none came down and needed these essentials on my watch), I slipped out of the Sullivan Hotel and into the descending dark of twilight.

And there on the porch, her cigarette glowing at the end as she took a deep inhale, was Tommie.

"Right on time," she said, flicking the ash off the end of the cigarette as she straightened and smiled at me. Her long, lanky body was wearing the hell out of a pinstripe suit jacket and wide-legged, tailored pants, a plain black tie loose at her neck. Her gaze was intense as she held mine, but her smile was utterly genuine. She was happy to see me.

I still hadn't worked up the courage to take a break and find Kane that day. I needed to talk to her about getting the lock changed back on my room, but I just couldn't bear the thought of facing her. Not now. Not yet. I'd talked with Gwen, and I was going to camp out on her couch in her room that night, give me a little more time to come to terms with all this.

Cowardly, I know. But I just felt that if I saw Kane right now, when it was still all so new, it'd be more harmful than helpful.

I was still raw inside from the previous night. I didn't need to pour salt in that wound *quite* yet.

Again, thoughts of Kane swirled in my head as I returned Tommie's smile. I tried, valiantly, to push Kane out of my head. I repeated what I'd told myself all day: Kane had Melody, Kane did not want me. But it's not as if I could just flip a switch.

And now, what I was feeling for Tommie was so tangled up in what I'd felt for Kane. In what I still felt for her.

I sighed out into the dark, my breath forming a mist ahead of me in the cold twilight. Tommie stepped forward, her brow furrowed as she cupped her fingers around my elbow, squeezing gently.

"Are you all right?" she asked me, her voice a low growl.

Not really, I thought. But I lied and told her: "yes."

Together, we walked away from the Sullivan Hotel, and toward her Mustang, parked at the far right edge of the almost-full gravel parking lot that sprawled in front of the hotel.

I glanced back over my shoulder at the massive red building. The Sullivan Hotel brooded on the edge of that cliff face, overlooking the sea. It was so hauntingly beautiful with its columns and stories and bright red stones, and I should have known from the moment that I arrived that this building would spell trouble for me.

But it was turning into a *nice* sort of trouble at least, I thought, as Tommie made an elegant little bow and pulled the car door open for me.

I folded into the passenger seat, and in an instant, Tommie was seated behind the wheel, flexing her shoulders and wrapping her fingers around the wheel.

"I park the boat at the harbor in town," she told me, turning the key in the ignition. The engine revved to life.

We slid out onto the road, the gravel spinning away from the back wheels as the car moved quickly through the encroaching darkness, down to Eternal Cove.

The old trees along the main street of Eternal Cove were all decked out in orange lights for Halloween, all of the shops full of window displays featuring witches and werewolves and cauldrons and pumpkins. Surprisingly, though every other character or emblem of Halloween was on display in the shop windows…I didn't see a single vampire.

"Down this way," said Tommie, parking the Mustang in an empty spot in front of the liquor store. The store, "Eternal Cove Spirits," was brightly lit and still open—the only shop on the entire main street that was. I stepped up and out of the Mustang and took

Tommie's arm when she proffered it to me, because—of course—she was almost instantly around the other side of the car. It was such a smooth motion, how she offered me her arm, how I didn't even hesitate or think about it. Mine had slid into hers like we'd done this before.

We walked down to the harbor. Even from the dock, you could hear the eerie (and yet, oddly beautiful) cadence of the ship's pulleys hitting their masts. It was beautiful, haunting music that seemed to merge with the water lapping against the pillars of the deck.

Tommie hopped down to one of the small rowboats tied to the dock, offering her hand up to me. She helped me down without a word, her hands lingering at my waist, helping me settle onto one of the seats in the rowboat. She untied the mooring line and pushed off from the dock with her foot, and then we were quietly pulling through the water as she rowed us with smooth, even strokes toward the sailboats.

There was a rope ladder that hung down from the side of one of the nearest sailboats, and this was the one that Tommie was aiming for. It was mostly white, as were all of the sailboats, but there was a thin line of red that was painted around the edge of the boat, and there on the back end of the boat, were two looping, cursive words.

"*The Song*?" I asked, glancing at Tommie. "Is that your boat?"

"Yes," she said, her jaw working as she pulled the oars again. She didn't elaborate on the name.

When we arrived at the boat, Tommie threaded the mooring line through the floating anchor, pulling the little rowboat up alongside *The Song*. She tugged on the rope ladder, drawing the rowboat even closer, and then she inclined her head toward the ladder.

"Ladies first," she said with a wolfish grin, and I returned the smile, standing uncertainly in the rocking rowboat. I put out my hand, steadying myself with the rope ladder, and then I put my foot in the first rung.

Climbing up a rope ladder *sounds* a lot easier than it actually is, especially in a dress, but I managed to get myself up and into the boat without making too much of a fool out of myself. Tommie scaled the rope ladder like she'd been doing it her entire life, and was right behind me and in the boat before I could even blink.

"All right," she said, walking forward to the ship's wheel, and patting the controls that included, I realized, an engine. "We'll use this to get out," she said, jerking her thumb toward the open water beyond the harbor. "And then it's wind all the way," she said, staring up at the small mast.

She sounded breathless, and more than a little affectionate, as she gazed up at the mast of the boat. She loved this boat, I realized, as Tommie started the motor and held onto the wheel, which wasn't really a wheel…it reminded me of the controls in an airplane. But as she pushed a lever forward and the ship sprang slowly to life, her fingers moved over the controls and gripped the wheel as gently as you'd grip a lover.

"I've had this boat for about half a century," said Tommie then, yelling a little to be heard over the engine. "It's meant the world to me," she said, worrying at the edge of her lip, and completely confirming what I'd thought. "For a time," she said, then, casting me a sideways glance, "I even slept on here rather than at the hotel."

"Why?" I asked in surprise.

Tommie grimaced again, her jaw working. "Kane and I..." she said then, wincing as she said the name. "We've not always seen eye to eye," she finished gravely.

"Do you care to elaborate?" I asked, leaning against the boat's railing. She cast me a wry smile and shook her head.

"Not really," she said, turning the boat a little so that it maneuvered between two other ships.

And then we were out into the almost still waters of the open ocean, the sunset behind us, over the land, painting the sky in purples, oranges, golds...it was breathtaking. But that still didn't distract from the fact that Tommie was being purposefully evasive.

"I fell in love with someone once," said Tommie, then. She was so quiet that I almost couldn't hear her over the roar of the engine, but I inched forward, mesmerized, and stood right next to her. She had a faraway look in her eye as she gazed out to sea, but then she shook her head, glanced at me. "I loved her utterly," she said with a sad smile and shrug, "but Kane loved her, too, and I never had a chance. I tried, believe me. We both did. But she wanted Kane."

The wind that roared past us, brought on by the swiftness of the boat, tossed her words away from me as I wrapped my arms around myself again and leaned against her.

"I'm sorry," I told her. "That's hard. There's no winning in that."

She glanced down at me again, her features softening as she wrapped an arm around my waist, pulling me closer.

"It doesn't matter anymore. I've spent so much of my life trying to forget her, and it was so much harder to do that than I thought it should be. But I've forgotten her now. Because I'm getting a chance with you."

I gazed up at her with wide eyes, tasting the salt of the ocean, and—in that moment—tasting Tommie as she leaned down and gently brushed her lips over mine.

The sailboat turned, and we began to make our way up the coast. With Tommie's strong arm around my waist (and my arm wrapping around hers, too), I didn't notice the cold of the air so much. Not that Tommie was warm (she was practically freezing to the touch), but there was something about having her hold me so tightly. I felt warm, even though I wasn't.

Ahead, through the darkness, rose the Sullivan Hotel.

The moon was edging out from behind clouds overhead—a gibbous moon that hung, almost full, in the cloudbank. It shed enough light to perfectly see the hotel by…from the ocean, it was such an impressive structure. It sprawled up on the cliff face like something out of a horror novel, with its red stone walls that, in the moonlight, looked almost bloody.

"Home sweet home," Tommie remarked with a wry chuckle. She groaned, then. "I can't wait for this Conference to be over. I'm used to being mostly by myself, having more independence…I have to be nailed down to all of these terrible meetings about things I just don't care about." She sighed out for a long moment and then began to brake the boat slowly. She turned off the ignition once the boat stood still. "I've never cared about most of the things that Kane cares about," said Tommie then, a snarl almost in her voice. I glanced at her in surprise.

"She wants this whole nicey-nice vampire culture," said Tommie then, taking off her suit jacket and laying it over the captain's chair situated behind the wheel. "She's trying to gather together all of the vampires who care about humans. But there aren't honestly that many of them. No offense," she told me with a grimace as gooseflesh began to appear on my arms. It was so strange to hear her talk about *humans* like that…like she wasn't one. Which…she probably wasn't anymore, since was a vampire. It was still the oddest thing.

"So…vampires mostly don't like humans?" I asked, feeling discomfort move through me. Tommie glanced sharply my way.

"Well. That's a nice way of putting it, I suppose," she said and sighed, gesturing overhead. "But let's not talk about stuff like this."

"It's kind of important that I know, really, considering where I'm working right now," I pointed out stubbornly.

Tommie folded her arms in front of her, her mouth going into a thin, stubborn light, just visible by the faint remnants of light along the horizon. "Bluntly put, most vampires wish that humans were enslaved into nice, easy blood bank type facilities."

I stared at her.

Tommie shrugged. "There aren't that many vampires out there. But there are fringe groups that are actually vying for that future. The Sullivans represent the polar opposite. Every one of the Sullivans believes that human beings, what we evolved from, deserve to live out their lives and be protected. It is not a popular opinion among our kind. That's what banded us together…after the love of women," she said, her lips tugging up at the edges.

"So…wow," I said, and then my legs buckled under me, and I sat down in the captain's chair, stunned. I blinked up at her. "Wow," I repeated, suddenly at a loss for words.

Tommie shrugged again. "Honestly, it's nothing to worry about. The factions of vampires who want to subjugate humans are fringe groups. Just like the KKK…it's not a *lot* of people who think that way, just some, thankfully. It's the same with vampires."

"That's still kind of terrifying," I muttered, rubbing at my arms and shivering.

Tommie knelt down in front of me smoothly, searching my eyes as she cupped my hands with gentle fingers. "Are you all right?" she asked.

"Not really," I told her truthfully, searching her gaze. "Tell me the truth: are there vampires from that fringe group at the Conference? At the Sullivan Hotel *right now*?"

"Yes," said Tommie instantly, her jaw working. "But there are treaties in effect that they cannot break, and none would be stupid enough to do so. If the treaties put in place during the Conference are broken, the vampire or vampires who break them are put to death. There is no trial, no excuse. There would never be any violence committed by vampires during the Conference—the punishment is too immovable and swift."

"Well that makes me feel a *little* better," I muttered, rubbing absent-mindedly at my neck and the healing wounds there as I took a deep breath.

"Come," said Tommie then with a small smile, standing and holding tightly to my hands as she pulled me up. "Come look at the stars."

There's so much light pollution on land, that—even if you're camping at one of the most remote places—there's a lot of starlight that's lost to the light of men. But out here, on the ocean, even though we weren't *that* far out from shore, the cascade of stars overhead immediately took my breath away. The long, bright line of the milky way practically pulsed with starlight, and as I stared overhead (my mouth open because I was in awe), Tommie wrapped her arm tightly around my waist, and I felt my body drawn to hers, leaning back against her.

"Tommie, it's *beautiful*," I managed to whisper to her. I felt her chest rumble in a chuckle behind me, and then Tommie brushed her cold mouth to the top of my head.

"Not nearly as beautiful as you," she quipped then. I felt the blush rising in me, and then I was turning of my own accord toward her, pressing myself against her, wrapping my arms around her waist.

Behind Tommie was the Sullivan Hotel, rising above us on the cliff face, and the long stretch of beach beneath the hotel glimmered in the moonlight. It was almost as bright outside as daytime because of the starlight and moonlight, and every little thing was visible.

As I reached up to kiss Tommie, as I felt drawn and pulled to her, my eyes flitted to the beach, only for a heartbeat.

And my heart skipped a beat at that moment. Because there was a figure on the beach. Someone was walking in the moonlight.

There were hundreds of people checked into the Sullivan Hotel right now, and the figure on the beach could have been any one of them. But I knew it wasn't.

I knew it was Kane. She was alone, walking the beach like she always did, lost deep in thought.

At that moment, as if she felt my eyes on her, the figure on the beach paused and stopped at the edge of the water. She turned toward us.

And I knew that Kane saw us, saw Tommie and me out on the water together, in each other's arms.

I shouldn't have cared. But, in that moment, I did. I felt my heart split into two pieces. I didn't know what to do, but I felt my body react, and I just let it.

I stepped away from Tommie.

She glanced at me in surprise, still holding onto my hands. Her head went to the side quizzically, and then she glanced over her shoulder, at the spot that I was staring at on the shore.

At Kane.

"Rose," she said then heavily, turning back to me with a quick shake of her head. "What—"

"It's nothing," I told her, biting my lip, my words tense and sharp. I stepped closer to her again, and—almost aggressively—I wrapped my arms around her waist.

I reached up, wrapped my fingers around the back of her neck, and I drew her down to me for a kiss.

She tasted of cigarette smoke and coffee, her lips soft and cool to the touch, her kiss utterly sensual and irresistible. She drank of me deeply, and my body responded as I carefully shut down my thoughts.

All I wanted to do was feel. And for a long moment, that strategy worked. I didn't think about Kane at all as I kissed Tommie, and I didn't dare look over Tommie's shoulder again, to see what the woman on the shore was doing. I focused wholly and utterly on Tommie, and I kissed her deeply.

But when we broke apart, when Tommie searched my gaze questioningly, I couldn't clamp down on the thoughts anymore, and one lone one found its way into my heart:

Kane. The pain in Kane's face as she turned away from us, only last night.

What was I doing? I felt so much for Kane, and I was trying so hard with Tommie.

Was I utterly doomed to be unhappy forever? Why couldn't I just stay in the moment, concentrate utterly on Tommie? Why did Kane keep coming up when I knew that I could never have her, that we could never be together? I was torturing myself, and I was becoming very quickly frustrated with myself.

Overhead, the Sullivan Hotel sat impassive on the cliff, life moving through it and not touching it.

This far out to sea, the building crouched, silent, brooding and uncaring.

The stars overhead were just as cold. And in front of me, Tommie's body was chill to the touch.

I held her hand tightly. I tried to pull my focus away from the shore.

And Kane, distant on the beach, turned and curved away from me as she walked away.

"How can we be out of milk?" I asked Gwen. I almost followed that up with *I didn't think vampires drank milk*, but I stopped myself just in time.

Gwen still didn't know *what*, exactly, our employers were. And it was probably best for her if it was kept that way.

At the very least, it was less stressful assuming you were working for human beings.

"Molly gave me the list, and we're out of milk," said Gwen with a shrug, tossing me a small notebook that bore our cook's writing across the top: *Kitchen Notes.* "And you've been pretty mopey today, so I thought you'd like to go grocery shopping with me, get you out of the hotel. Because we could totally stop by the coffee shop…" Gwen trailed off, cocking her head to the side as she wrinkled her nose and took me in. "I mean, it's your day *off*, Rose…don't tell me you're just going to stay in here? It's not like I don't like having you in my room every minute that you're not working…" she said, spreading her hands with a brow raised. "But you definitely need some outdoor time. Or…*something*." She pursed her lips and put her hands on her hips. "I mean, it's *gorgeous* out. It's the perfect fall day. You shouldn't waste it."

I shrugged a little, playing with the hem of my sweater. Its true: I was in a bad mood today. Gwen was being utterly wonderful, letting me stay in her room, but it wasn't the biggest room in the world, and she was right: every moment I wasn't working I *was* in here. I knew my best friend valued her alone time.

But I still hadn't worked up the courage to go see Kane about getting my lock changed. I had somewhat hoped that it would just happen all by itself without any interference from me, that Kane would remember that I needed my lock changed back and would order it done.

That way, I could avoid seeking her out. I could avoid talking to her. I could avoid seeing her.

Okay, so that was totally cowardly. But every single time I *thought* about Kane, my heart broke all over again. I couldn't really imagine what would happen if I saw her face to face, if I saw that sorrow in her expression, in her bright blue eyes as she gazed at me, seeing to the very deepest parts of me.

God, this was such a mess.

"What about Tommie? Why aren't you with her today?" asked Gwen innocently, sitting down on the couch next to me. I drew my legs up under my skirt and sighed.

"She's in a meeting for the Conference all day. We're going to do something tonight," I told her.

"Like what…" She drew out the words, her brows raised. I shrugged.

"I'm not sure. Maybe another boat ride. It was really lovely last night," I said, which was the truth. But the beauty and majesty of the evening and the countless number of stars overhead had been somewhat dampened by my spotting Kane on the beach. And, immediately, being unable to control the strong feelings that surged through me.

"Come to Eternal Cove with me," said Gwen in a strong tone that brooked no argument. She got up quickly, stretching overhead. "Seriously. You can't stay cooped up in here all day. You're making me feel all antsy. And two people grocery shopping is *so* much faster than one," she cajoled, waggling her brows at me as she chuckled. When I raised a single brow at her and smiled, she went for broke: "I'll buy you a pumpkin *latte*," she sang.

At that point, I just felt silly. My best friend was doing everything in her power to make me feel better, and was letting me stay in her room because I couldn't work up the courage to speak to our boss.

I could manage a trip to town. It was the *least* I

could do.

"Okay, okay," I chuckled, rising. "How can I refuse a pumpkin latte?"

"I thought you were going to say how could you refuse *me*?" she asked with a small pout, but then Gwen chuckled and wrapped her arms around my shoulders, squeezing tightly before taking a step back. "Do me a big favor before we head out?" she asked. The words were purposefully light and innocent, and my eyes narrowed at that.

"What?" I asked.

"Can you talk to Kane about switching your lock back? Or giving you a key to your room?" she asked. Her brows were raised, but she was very carefully watching my expression, waiting for my reaction.

It was stupid that I hadn't already asked her for these things—it should have been the *first* thing I did. I knew that. But still, when she said the word *Kane*, my stomach dropped away from me.

But I needed my room back. It wasn't fair to Gwen.

"Yeah," I said, keeping my voice light. "I can do that," I smiled at her, realizing how fake it probably looked, but I was doing the best I could. "Why don't you get dressed?" I asked, gesturing to her pajamas, "and I'll meet you downstairs at the front desk? Kane's probably still in her office getting ready for the meeting," I said, hazarding a guess. I didn't know exactly where she was, but it was as good a place as any to start looking for her. And if she *wasn't* in her office, at least I could say that I'd tried to find her. "I'll talk to her," I said, my tongue suddenly dry. I cleared my throat, pressed my already sweating palms to my skirted thighs.

I could do this.

I moved quickly out of Gwen's bedroom and down the spiral staircase before I could change my mind. I walked past vampires milling in the hallways, socializing and meeting on the landings as they congregated around the comfortable couches set up there as social areas. Some of them flicked their eyes to me (*fresh meat*, I thought), but I purposefully did not look their way, and as I walked down the floors, moving toward Kane's office, I became more and more lost in my thoughts and worries.

I'd knock on Kane's door only once, I decided. And if I didn't hear anything inside in a heartbeat (or so), I'd turn around and make my way immediately back up to Gwen's bedroom, and I could tell her that I'd tried, but there'd been no one there.

Hey, it was a cowardly plan, admittedly: but at least I was going to *try*.

When I reached Kane's office, I stopped at the door, raising my hand to the antique wood. All of my plans crumbled in that moment, because I heard a low, muted woman's voice inside.

There was someone in there.

Kane.

I pressed my palm flat to the door, felt the wood beneath my already too-warm skin as I felt the blush erupt in my skin.

I took a deep breath, every inch of my body shaking. And then I curled my hand into a fist, lifted it from the wood and knocked once, quietly against the door.

There was silence from the other side for a heartbeat. And then came the smooth, soft growl:

"come." That single word knocked the breath out of me, made every atom in my body turn toward her. Because it was Kane's voice on the other side of that door.

I took a deep breath, steadied myself against the doorknob as I somehow found a few more scraps of courage inside of me. And then I opened the door, letting myself into the dark room. I shut the door behind me, waiting for my eyes to adjust to the dark for a moment. Her scent assaulted me, the intoxicating, cool scent of jasmine, vanilla and spice. It seemed to merge with the old wood of the walls and desk, the pungent aroma of old books that lined the walls behind her.

"Rose." The single word came from the darkness in the room, from the other side of the room.

And that single word broke my heart.

Kane's voice was low and strong, but in that single syllable, the syllable of my name, her voice broke at the end. It was almost inaudible, how her voice cracked at the end of it, but the room was so still and quiet, I heard it anyway. Her voice, normally so throaty and low and strong, had broken.

My eyes adjusted, and I took in the broad, antique desk, took in the woman seated behind it.

She was wearing a suit and tie, as always. Her long, white-blonde hair was pulled back into a severe ponytail, and her bright blue eyes were piercing me through as she rose slowly, ascending like an angel as she stood, straight and tall, behind the desk, one hand gripping the edge of the desk like she needed to hold tightly to it in order to keep from collapsing.

She stared at me, and her mouth downturned, softly and slowly, into a frown.

"What can I do for you?" she asked, her voice gentle. I stared at her, tried to take a deep breath, my heart pounding inside of me.

It couldn't be like this, every time we saw one another. We lived in the same house, and it was a very big house, but she was my boss, and I was her employee, and that meant we'd have to see each other often. And it couldn't be like this every time.

I couldn't bear this, every time. And I didn't think she could, either. I took a deep breath, straightened my shoulders, and looked past her gaze, at the bookshelf behind her.

"My lock...could it be changed back? Or could I get the keys to the one that was put in? I'm staying with Gwen right now, since Melody changed the lock on my door, but I think I'm crowding Gwen," I said, surprised at how calm my voice sounded. My gaze flicked back to her, and I hoped that she couldn't see in the dark how my eyes roved over her body.

We were about ten feet apart, but it was obvious to me, in that moment, that even that distance wasn't enough. I could feel the pull of her body tugging me closer, and it was taking every single ounce of strength within me to resist it.

I was pulled to her like the tides are pulled to shore. I didn't understand why, and in that moment, I hated it. I wanted this to be simple—I wanted to be able to come with her with a simple request like a key to my room. But even this was complicated, this simple standing, ten feet apart.

I wanted to taste her, I realized, as I stared at her, as I stared at her full lips, downturning into a frown at the mere sight of me. And I would never be able to taste her again.

We stood like that, tense and hard, each body curling away from the other, tension crackling between us like electricity racing through a wire.

"Yes," she said heavily, finally. She pulled open the top drawer next to her, and took out a key ring that contained two brass keys. "I'm sorry for all this trouble," she said then, the words low and long. She breathed out, held the keys out to me in the palm of her hand.

I didn't want to cross that space between us to stand in front of her. I didn't want to hold out my hand to her, to chance the moment that skin might brush against skin. I have self-control, I have strength, but this was something outside those bounds. The want and need that roared through me, the tug of gravity that was Kane, standing behind the desk, was otherworldly.

I took a step forward. Two. I took three and four, and then I was standing right in front of the desk. I was shaking, as I held out my hand to her.

Kane took a deep breath, staring down at that hand, and then she set the keys on top of the desk. She reached out with long fingers, and she curled them around my wrist so softly and gently that when her skin touched mine, I almost cried out.

It was almost painful, when her skin met mine. There was such a jolt of longing that roared through me that I felt faint. My breathing intensified, my heart roared through me, and then somehow, impossibly, Kane was bending to me, bending forward in a soft, sweeping bow.

She turned my hand over, and curving forward with cold grace, she pressed her cool mouth to my palm.

"Please don't," I whispered, and then she was gazing up at me from that position, bent elegantly forward, her mouth against my palm. Her piercing blue gaze held me to the spot, and there was such a shocking amount of desire in that gaze, such power in those two blue eyes, that I felt my resolve peel away from me like petals. I wanted to crawl across the desk for her, wrap my arms around her, savagely pull her to me and kiss her like I'd never kissed anyone before. Like this was the first and best kiss of my entire life.

Her body called to me, and my own answered. And there was nothing to be done about any of it.

But I resisted. And she did, too, because she regretfully straightened, curling her body upward and away from me like it was the most painful thing she'd ever done.

"I'm sorry," she said, the words pain-filled and husky. She picked up the keys and set them in my palm, and her fingers lingered as I stood there woodenly, my eyes filling with tears.

I didn't understand what was between us. I didn't understand why I was so drawn to her. But I was. She was everything that I'd ever wanted, the woman that I had dreamed of my entire life.

In that single moment, I had somehow betrayed Tommie, I knew. But with Tommie, I was betraying Kane.

Wasn't I?

I stared at her in confusion, my eyes filling with tears. I held my breath, willing the tears to stop, but a single hot drop spilled out of my right eye and traced its way down my cheek.

I couldn't hold it in anymore.

"What are you doing to me?" I asked then,

brokenly, holding the keys tightly to my chest, curling my fingers tightly around the freezing metal. "Why are you doing this?" I asked, the words breaking at the ends.

"Please, Rose," she whispered, her voice shaking as she braced herself against the edge of the desk. Her gaze raked over me and fixed itself to the top of her desk. Her eyes had looked hunted. "I would rather die than hurt you," she whispered.

"You're hurting me," I told her.

We stared at one another, then. She shook her head, her violently blue eyes closed to me. When she opened them, she stared at the surface of her desk. She did not look at me.

"Please," she said then, taking a quavering, deep breath. "Please go. I'm sorry."

I turned on my heel, and somehow I found the strength to make my way across the room, to open the door and push my body out of it. I stumbled down the hallway, and I found a restroom, its heavy oaken door hardly able to be opened, but I managed to tug it toward me, and I let myself into the old bathroom, holding myself up against the wall.

This was crazy. There was something between Kane and I that defied conventional ideas, that defied what I'd thought the world could be like. It was uncontrollable, the connection between us, and somehow—impossibly—it had to be controlled.

If I was going to begin a relationship with Tommie, I had to commit to her one hundred percent. I had never cheated, and I would never cheat, but there was such a draw to Kane that it seemed almost impossible for me to halt the maddening crescendo of need that I felt for that woman.

I took a deep breath. I just had to concentrate on Tommie. I had to concentrate on Tommie wholeheartedly, and then maybe…maybe I could forget about Kane.

I laughed at myself in that moment, laughed as tears traced their way down my cheeks.

How could I *hope* to forget the maddening, gorgeous woman when our paths would cross, *every single day*?

This was all so impossible and pain-filled. But, somehow, I had to keep going.

I washed my face carefully with cold water in the sink, drying it on the paper towels from the dispenser as I stared at my reflection in the mirror. I took a couple more deep breaths, and then I left the restroom, pasted a pleasant expression on my face and found my way back to Gwen's room.

"Mission accomplished," I told her, my voice cracking a little at the end, but I bit my lip and tried a smile as I held out my hand with the key ring in the center of my palm. "Great, right?" I asked her. She was drying her hair from the shower she'd just taken, and she looked suspicious as she stared at me with a single brow raised, but she nodded, folding the towel over the ends of her hair that were already curling.

"Yeah, that's good," she said, frowning. She paused. "Rose, are you all right?"

"Fine," I lied again. It was becoming a regular occurrence, these lies, but I took another deep breath and attempted a smile.

We drove together down to Eternal Cove and found the only grocery store situated off the main road. It was called Paul Whitby's Grocery, and looked like it'd existed in Eternal Cove for longer than the town itself had existed. It was also tiny (though well stocked and maintained, I thought, what with having worked at a grocery store for many, many years), but it didn't need to have exotic ingredients.

The shopping list was not that long or extensive that Molly, the cook, wanted for the hotel. We were apparently out of milk and pancake mix (it was an almost amusing idea to me, the thought of vampires ever eating pancakes. I would assume that the pancake mix was mostly for Sullivan Hotel's staff of humans), and lettuce and tomatoes. By the time we were loading up the car, it was already late afternoon, and we took a quick detour to the coffee shop, ordering our lattes to go.

"I need batteries for my camera," said Gwen thoughtfully as she blew on the surface of her latte, the steam curling up around her already too-curly hair. "For the dance on Friday!" she said with a wink. "It needs to be documented, all of that fanciness. I even ordered a dress online. I think you'll like it—"

I was off in my own little world at that point, but this statement brought me back to reality. "You ordered a dress?" I repeated, blinking. "Why?"

"We're *all* going to the dance, Rose," she said, her brows rising. "Everyone in Eternal Cove is talking about it—they're all going to go. Not much happens around here, so Kane made the dance open to the public. And that includes us."

I stared at her with an open mouth. My first thought was that all of the townsfolk of Eternal Cove would be vulnerable to vampire attack…but then I remembered (for the millionth time) that the treaty for the Conference was in place, and that the vampires couldn't hunt while they were here.

But the reason I clung to that thought was the too-painful one that was beginning to make my heart *actually* hurt:

I'd have to go.

"Well," I said, glancing at the barista who was still making my latte. He was pumping the whipped cream on top, currently. "We don't all *have* to go."

She pursed her lips, huffing out a small sigh. "You won't come?"

I ran my hand through my hair, taking a deep breath. "There's no reason for me to show up," I told her, taking the latte from the barista. Outside, it was beginning to darken, autumn storm clouds roiling along the edges of the horizon again. It was a stormy autumn that they had in Maine, but it seemed to be much worse, concentrated as it was around Eternal Cove.

It matched my mood perfectly.

"I mean, it'd be a great date for you and Tommie," said Gwen innocently, raising her eyes as we both turned and made our way toward the coffee shop door. "Trust me," she said with a slight eye roll," you're going to be very bored for good date spots pretty soon. In all of Eternal Cove, there's this coffee shop, the tiny movie theater that gets one new movie every *month*, and an Italian diner. You're going to be wishing for opportunities like this in about a month. And you know how far Portsmouth is."

"I don't think I'm going to tire of Eternal Cove's dating options," I muttered, worrying my finger at the rim of the to-go lid. I traced the recycling symbol pressed there. "It's just…the problem is *Kane*, Gwen. It's really hard with Kane being there. And, I assume, since she owns the hotel that she's going to be at the dance." I took a deep breath and shook my head. "I don't think I can be in the same room as her for a while."

My best friend gazed at me with raised eyebrows. "I thought it was all Tommie all the time now," she said flatly.

"God, you make me sound so flippant," I muttered, feeling an ache roar through my bones. I *wasn't* flippant. I was confused, and those were two very, very different things.

"You're not flippant," said Gwen soothingly. "I just don't think you know what you want."

"I want Kane," I blurted out, "but I can't have her."

We'd made our way out to the coffee shop steps, and Gwen paused now, staring at me with wide eyes.

It was true, I realized as I took a deep breath.

It was utterly true.

"Rose," said Gwen quietly, searching my eyes as she leaned forward and gripped my arm, "Kane has Melody now. You wouldn't...you wouldn't ask Kane to cheat on her?" she asked, her voice almost a whisper now.

"That's horrific," I muttered, tears filling my eyes. "How can you even ask me that? No," I replied, after a deep breath. "I would never do that."

"Then what *are* you going to do?" she asked me quietly, searching my gaze.

"I mean, what choice do I have, Gwen?" I asked her, gripping my cup so tightly that the lid popped off. I pushed it back down all around the rim as we walked back to the car. I took an impulsive sip of my far-too-hot latte. "I'm going to be miserable, and I'm going to try to forget what I want, and I really *like*

Tommie," I told her too quickly, stumbling over the words. "And that's enough to help me try and forget." God, it sounded so terrible, saying those words out loud. But it was the truth, whether I wanted it to be or not. "I'm not using Tommie," I said quickly, glancing sidelong at Gwen. "I mean…I feel like I've known Kane all my life, and I feel that way with Tommie, too. It's different, but I still do care about her. I think I could grow to love her," I said softly. "It's just…it's just not like it is with Kane."

Gwen unlocked Moochie's doors and hopped up into her van. She shrugged a little, shoving the key into the ignition. "It doesn't have to be this complicated, Rose. I understand that you had a thing for Kane, but you never actually did much with her, and now Tommie's all over you. I don't understand why you're throwing something so good to the wind."

I climbed up into her van, too, feeling hurt. There was no way that I could possibly explain what I felt for Kane to Gwen. It'd sound too esoteric or gushy or weird. *We have a connection* really didn't cover everything I felt for Kane. What Gwen said was true—but my feelings weren't lying.

"I'm not throwing anything away," I said softly. "I know what I have with Tommie, and that's why I'm going on dates with her, and…and…" I spluttered, working my hand in a circle as I tried to explain myself. I was frustrated at how I couldn't articulate the connection I felt with Kane, and I was frustrated that I couldn't properly convey to my best friend that I *wasn't* taking advantage of Tommie. I *did* care about her, it just wasn't how I cared about Kane.

But I could *get* there with Tommie. Couldn't I?

Gwen started the engine and nosed the van out

onto the rush-hour traffic of the main street of Eternal Cove. Which mostly consisted of three other vehicles idling at the stoplight with us and nothing else.

It was already starting to get dark as we turned the nose of the van toward the Sullivan Hotel, beginning up the steep road toward the top of the hill.

Gwen gritted her teeth and muttered an expletive under her breath. I glanced at her in surprise, but she was looking in her rearview mirror.

"Some jackass is riding me," she muttered, pushing Moochie's gas pedal down as far as it could go. The van was a surprisingly good vehicle for how ancient it was, but it could only do so much, especially on such a steep incline. We were going twenty-five miles an hour, and the van's engine was roaring. This was the absolute best it was capable of.

I glanced in my side mirror. The vehicle behind us was a large Hummer. It was already too dark to make out the driver or the passenger, but then it no longer mattered, because the driver floored his Hummer (which was much better equipped to deal with sharp inclines than Gwen's poor van), and swerved around us to pass us.

"About time," Gwen muttered, letting off on the gas a little to let the guy pass.

But he didn't pass.

"Gwen," I began, turning to look at her, intent on saying something else entirely, but I don't remember what that was…

Because, instead, I screamed as the Hummer broadsided us.

Gwen had been driving with only her left hand on the wheel. With the weight—and force—of the Hummer, the wheel went spinning, and so did the van.

We were at a hairpin turn in the road, and the van immediately tumbled off the side of it. Because Moochie is heavy, too, it didn't go too far. We were only in the ditch, the seatbelts pinning us to the seats, Gwen staring at the ceiling in a daze. The driver's side door was crushed inward, but Moochie had been built like a tank—Gwen must have hit her head, but there wasn't any blood.

I was fine.

Pure instinct and adrenaline took over as I snapped out of my seatbelt. "Gwen?" I whispered, then said it a bit louder, shaking her arm just a little. Gwen blinked blearily and turned her head to glance at me.

Down the road, the Hummer had pulled over. I could see both the driver's side door and the passenger door opening and shutting, and two people running toward us in Moochie's headlights.

*At least they have the decency to help*, I thought, as I undid Gwen's seatbelt. All I could think about was Moochie combusting into flames—through the windshield, I could see how badly pushed inwards Moochie's hood was. We'd hit a tree, which is what had stopped our trajectory. If we'd been going faster, I don't know what would have become of us.

"Gwen, please, are you all right to move?" I asked her, panting as I twisted myself and rose to my knees in the passenger seat. My passenger side door was wedged against another tree, so there was no getting out that way. We'd have to take Moochie's back door out, which meant Gwen needed to be able to get out of her seat. But what if she had a spinal injury?

Another car passed us and the Hummer, driving slowly up the road. I glanced up in surprise, looking for the two people who had exited the Hummer…but I didn't see them.

My stomach turned at that. First off, there was no way that the Hummer hadn't seen us when he was trying to merge back into the lane. Not unless he was drunk, and how was that possible so early in the afternoon/evening? And with such an expensive car, it would seem that you'd want to be careful.

No, honestly…it had seemed deliberate.

I tried to swallow my suspicions and I turned my entire attention onto Gwen, but my skin on the back of my neck was crawling.

Things didn't feel right. The Hummer's hazard lights were flashing in the darkness—Moochie's headlights had gone out.

Which, effectively, had plunged me and Gwen into darkness.

Because we weren't up on the top of the hill yet, and because the sun didn't set over the ocean, but over the land instead, we were in a pocket on the side of the hill that was much darker than it would have been elsewhere. This, also, gave me chills.

It was like this had been planned.

But what the hell *for*?

"Gwen, please wake up," I whispered, shaking her shoulder a little.

"I'm up, I'm up," she muttered, moaning a little as she reached up and brushed her fingertips against her forehead. "Oh, my God, what happened?" she asked, opening her eyes wide and taking in the damage. "Did I hit a deer?"

She couldn't remember. Maybe she hadn't seen, but if she *had* seen, was the loss of memory a sign of shock? I had no idea. If she was in shock, did that mean she had other injuries?

"No deer," I muttered, glancing out the windshield again. The Hummer sat on the side of the road, flashing away. And there was no sign of its occupants.

Something was very wrong.

"Are you hurt? Can you wiggle your fingers for me, move your legs? I think we have to go," I told her quickly, climbing over the center console of the van into the back where the groceries had spilled out of their paper bags, tomatoes and heads of lettuce rolling everywhere.

"Of *course* I can wiggle my damn fingers and toes," said Gwen testily. "What did we hit?"

"That Hummer hit us," I said, pointing out the windshield.

She stared at it in surprise, reaching for her seatbelt—which I'd already unbuckled. "It sideswiped us?" she muttered.

Okay, so this meant she probably wasn't in shock, right? That she could remember the Hummer had tried to pass us? "Yeah," I told her, biting my lip and glancing out the passenger side window of the van. "Look, Gwen, I think we really need to get out of here. In case…in case the engine explodes or something," I told her quickly.

I didn't want to tell her that I thought something nefarious was going on. Because what if it wasn't? Gwen had no idea currently that the Sullivan Hotel was full of, and run by, vampires, and I thought it best to keep it that way. If, at least, for a little while longer.

And, frankly, was it really my place to tell her? Kane hadn't seemed exactly eager to reveal that fact to me, either, and was forced to, only to save my life.

"Okay, okay," she wheezed, wincing as she climbed up onto her seat and then crawled over the center console to the back of the van with me. She slipped on a tomato and fell into me.

That's when I felt something wet against my hand when I reached out to steady her.

"Gwen, are you hurt?" I whispered, but she grunted at me, shaking her head.

"Dunno. Let's get out of here."

I lifted up my hand, and—even in the meager light—I could tell my palm was slick with blood.

"Gwen, I think you're hurt," I told her, my voice higher, but Gwen sighed at me and smiled a little tightly.

"Won't matter if Moochie explodes and turns us into hamburger," she told me, jerking her thumb toward the back doors. "Can you get those open from the inside? Do you remember how?" She was pressing her hand to her side, where I'd reached out and touched her. Her cardigan was black, but I could still make out the darkening stain that was soaking through her t-shirt beneath the cardigan.

"Um, um," I muttered, clenching my teeth and running my hands—one blood-stained and one not—over the back panel of the doors. Moochie was an *old* van, and they weren't exactly safety adept in the eighties, or whatever decade created Moochie. The back doors opened perfectly well from the outside, but inside there was a funky latch that you had to hold down while pressing outward.

Something hit the side of the van.

My heart leapt into my throat, and Gwen fell against me as the van rocked gently from side to side, the impact enough to have made two wheels on the left side leave the ground. There was only one small window in the rear of the van, and the two back doors had no windows. It was impossible to see what was outside, except through the windshield.

Which only showed the Hummer blinking, its headlights beaming on the pavement as fog began to move eerily across the road.

"What the hell was that?" asked Gwen, her voice high, too, as she gripped me tightly. "Are we stable? We're not near the cliffs, are we?"

We were, but we weren't far enough off the road to be in danger of falling over them. With shaking hands, I managed to undo the back latch of the doors, and then they were falling open.

We were in a ditch, and the wheels weren't exactly flush with straight ground. It could have been anything that had made the van move, including earth falling against the side of the van, but as I helped Gwen out, I looked at the driver's side of the van again.

There was a huge indent, like a meteor had fallen against the metal.

There was something out here with us.

And I knew it was vampires.

I'd been hunted once before, and that old fear merged with my new fear now, running together through my blood as it pounded in every vein of my body. I remembered the feeling of the teeth against my skin, remembered the feeling of the cold water covering my head as she dragged me down into the depths to drink me dry. How she had lured me out into the sea by faking that she was drowning. Because vampires were the most coldly intelligent predator of them all.

They were practically human.

"What's happening?" asked Gwen, holding her hand against her side as she began to pale in the darkness. "Rose—"

"We've got to go," I managed, gripping her free hand tightly and pulling her up and out of the ditch. I was operating on pure adrenaline now, adrenaline that made heaving my taller best friend out of the ditch behind me something I didn't even notice.

We were still far from the hotel, and we were just far enough away from the town that if we screamed, there wouldn't be a single soul who heard us.

Again, something that made me think this was planned. A little farther up or down the road, and there might be the hope of safety.

Well, we'd just have to get there then before we were caught. I turned to look over my shoulder, but all I saw was the Hummer's hi-beams, and Moochie's dead hulk practically on its side in the ditch.

"I think we should head up," I told Gwen, ignoring my instinct that downhill would be much easier.

Downhill was humans. Who might be able to help us, admittedly, but uphill? Uphill was vampires who cared about us and wanted us alive. Vampires who would be very, very pissed that their treaty had been broken.

If we could get to them, we'd be safe.

But that was a pretty big *if*.

I stared up and up and up that hill. Over the towering trees, the distant lights of the Sullivan Hotel were brightening the sky. But I couldn't see the hotel itself. If we went up the road, we'd be perfectly vulnerable, but there was the chance that a passing motorist would go by, and then we'd be able to flag them down (hopefully). If we went up through the trees and forested areas, cutting across the roads when we absolutely had to, we'd be less vulnerable, but there'd be no hope for help until we got within earshot of the Sullivan Hotel.

Gwen sagged against me just then, breathing out through her nose in a *whoosh.* I had to figure out what to do—and fast.

I glanced around, holding Gwen tightly around the waist as we began to ascend the hill through the trees. There was so much tight underbrush and thorns and branches that hadn't been cleared away probably since Eternal Cove had been settled. It was just light enough out that I could still make out the shapes of the trees. The encroaching fog from the ocean had already slunk into the woods, and everything kind of looked like a set of a horror movie.

I'm certain that being hunted by a vampire wasn't exactly helping my perception of the woods.

I kept glancing back over my shoulder. Gwen was losing a lot of blood, and her earlier awareness was beginning to slip from her. She kept trying to walk, though, and she kept trying to lean against me as little as possible. We doggedly kept marching up the hill, even when my skirt got caught on a branch so hard that it ripped when I couldn't untangle it, even when she fell against a tree and crumpled to the ground. I lifted her up, she tried to rise, and together, we kept going.

There was a sound to my left. It was innocuous, at first—I thought it might be a raccoon or a deer, rustling around in the brush, but I was also hyper-aware, and turned to look.

It was a human shadow I saw, moving away into the fog.

A vampire.

I hissed out my breath between my teeth and began limping farther to the right. I could hear the roar and crash of the ocean through the trees. Maybe it'd be easier out by the cliffs to try to make it up the hill anyway. At least I'd have a clearer view if someone came for us.

I stumbled out of the woods with Gwen, and we began to trudge up through the grasses. Now I could see the Sullivan Hotel, at least its roof, but it was still *so* far away. I thought we were closer than that.

I heard another sound of breaking branches in the woods. I figured that vampires could be pretty damn stealthy when they wanted to be.

Were they breaking branches on purpose?

To what end? To terrify us to death?

It was almost working.

I kept trying to keep my breath even, but it was difficult, carrying Gwen and also feeling the terror pump through me. What I was trying to concentrate on, holding it tightly in my heart, was my small spark of anger.

I was angry that they'd come after Gwen and I, I was angry that Gwen had gotten so hurt. I was angry that if anything happened to me, it would probably also happen to my best friend, who absolutely, positively deserved none of this. I should have told her that we worked for vampires, I should have told her everything. But I hadn't, and now she was going to die. We both were.

I took another deep breath and went a few more feet before the sound of breaking branches had grown so strong that I had to look.

There were two figures standing in the mist on

the edge of the woods. They darted into the shadows when I looked at them, but I'd seen them.

They were so close when they darted away. They could have lunged forward and grabbed both of us. But they didn't.

I took a deep breath and strayed even further into the grasses, toward a deer path on the edge of the cliff face. Far, far, far down below me, the roll and hiss of the surf hitting the beach was a soothing lull. The tide was coming in. Overhead, the moon swung low, and stars were beginning to pop out of the black-blue of the sky. It was, by all accounts, an utterly beautiful autumn night.

I didn't want to die.

I didn't want Gwen to die.

Not here. Not like this. Not now.

And not because of me.

A sob stuck in my throat, but I kept going, kept dragging Gwen along. She'd gone unconscious now, and she was leaning entirely on my shoulder, her feet dragging along behind us. I gripped her around the waist with such force that I was probably breaking a rib, but if I let even a little tension on my arm go now, I'd drop her entirely. I pushed her a little up further on my shoulder, trying to get her to drape over my shoulder and back, wondering if it'd be easier to carry her like that.

And out of the mist to our left again came two shadows, darting forward.

I stumbled to the right—far closer to the cliff face than I ever wanted to go. I took a deep breath, spreading my feet wide, and trying to take a crouching stance as I held Gwen tightly. Being this close to the edge was playing tricks with my head. Far down below, the ocean pounded the land in a constant rhythm that never stopped, the sound rushing like my blood through my body.

The two figures disappeared, and I glanced to my right. I was a single foot away from the edge.

It was then that I realized what they were trying to do.

They were herding us off the cliff face.

I took a deep breath as panic rolled through me, just like the adrenaline. They didn't want to drain us dry—they wanted us to fall to our deaths. But why? To make it look like an accident?

To not break the treaty? Technically?

I hated them so much in that moment. Why were they hunting us? They weren't even after us for our blood. Did they want us dead just for some heinous reason, or was there a colder one? Had someone put them up to this, and—if so—who wanted us dead?

God, there were at least a few vampires who didn't like me very much. I swallowed and tightened my hold around Gwen.

I was not going to be pushed off this cliff. If they wanted us dead, they were going to have to do it themselves. I began to walk toward the woods again.

And the figures came out of the shadows, close enough to see them.

One was a man, tall and burly with a big leather trench coat on. He had long, black hair pulled back into a ponytail. The other was a redheaded woman, wearing a long peacoat and tall boots.

Their hands were in their pockets, but in the darkness, I could still tell that they were smiling.

And that they had very sharp teeth.

They said nothing as they approached us. They didn't have to. Their intimidating presence pushed me back, but I refused to move. I stood as fastly as I could, holding tight to Gwen as my heart rose into my throat. There was nowhere for me to run. I wasn't going to leave my best friend behind, and I wasn't going to throw both of us off the cliff.

I stood still, and I tried to take deep, even breaths as terror poured through me.

"I'm sorry," I whispered then. To Gwen. To Tommie.

And to Kane.

I closed my eyes, took a deep breath and tried to brace myself against the pain that was going to be inevitable and final and absolute.

When nothing happened after a long moment, I screwed up enough courage to open my right eye.

The two vampires were turning to the right, their noses to the wind. They were sniffing the air, I realized, like they scented something.

It was so quick that if I hadn't been staring at the right one, the woman, I never would have believed that it happened. The woman was standing, hands deep into her coat pockets, her nose to the wind, and then she wasn't there anymore. She was rolling end over end, someone on top of her.

The man went down just as quickly. The fog and the darkness made watching things closely almost impossible, but I saw bits and pieces of them turning end over end in the dark, and I heard the man's snarl. It made the hair stand up on the back of my neck it was so savage and low, but then I heard another voice. A voice I recognized.

It was Kane there, Kane pinning the man down

to the earth by his throat, then. Everything had become stilled. She crouched over him, pinning him to the spot, her knee on his chest and pushing down with such force that I heard a rib break beneath her.

The man cried out in pain, but Kane tightened her hold on his massive neck, and he was silenced.

To the side, Tommie rose from the ground, holding the woman's hands behind her back in an elaborate corkscrew that couldn't have felt great for that woman. Tommie looked past the man, looked past Kane.

Her eyes fell on me, and if I hadn't been holding up Gwen, I would have taken a step back.

She looked utterly feral. Wild.

Dangerous.

"What did you do," Tommie hissed, and even though they were a distance away at this point, and her voice was soft and low, I still heard. The cold anger in the voice carried to where I stood with Gwen.

I glanced back at Kane, but Kane wasn't looking my way. She was bearing the full weight of her violently blue gaze down on the man on the ground.

"Who do you work for?" she asked then, her voice a growl that made me shiver. She loosened her grip of hands around the man's neck, but he shook his head.

And then, moving faster than my eyes could follow, the man rolled out from under Kane, rising in a fluid motion that I assume a tiger would make. Kane rolled over and landed on the balls of her feet in a crouch.

The man took one look over his shoulder before he bolted toward the tree line.

And Kane followed him like a lioness who was

about to fell her prey.

And she did.

Kane hit the man squarely in the back, and they rolled end over end before darting between the trees.

In the stillness and rush of the ocean below, the scuffle in the woods ended. I heard a great cracking sound.

Kane walked slowly out from between the trees. There was a ragged cut in her suit shirt (her jacket was nowhere to be seen), and through the hole in the shirt, I could clearly see the gaping wound in her stomach. But there was no blood that seeped out of that wound. It was clean and dry, just wet flesh peeled back and open.

And, as I watched it, as she prowled toward us, the wound began to knit together and heal itself, lacing itself up like a corset of flesh.

So much had just happened. So much. I wanted Kane to catch my eyes, to—with that one, simple glance—tell me that everything was all right now. That we were safe. But as I watched the wound knit up on Kane's stomach, I realized how much I didn't know about her. How much I didn't know about any of them.

So Kane did not look at me as she stalked past Gwen and I. She had eyes only for the woman Tommie held tightly.

Kane's gaze was more dangerous than I'd ever seen it before. Her eyes were narrowed, but in the darkness, I could still see them flashing with a deep, frozen rage. And as she approached the woman, the woman who bore the brunt of her cold and terrifying gaze, the woman fell to her knees, shaking.

"I'll tell you, I'll tell you," she whimpered, wincing away as Tommie tightened her grip on the woman's arms. She licked her lips, eyes darting from Kane, to me, back to Kane again. She looked terrified, but she opened her mouth. She said: "Darcy. It was Darcy."

Kane stopped as suddenly as if she'd run into an invisible wall. Darcy. Why was Darcy such a familiar name? It meant something, something terrible, but I couldn't think of what it reminded me of. Not yet.

Tommie glanced at Kane, her eyes own wide as she shook her head with a slow, measured rhythm. "That's impossible," said Tommie, tightening her grip on the vampire's arms again. I heard something snap wetly in the vampire, but the vampire woman made no sound other than grinding her teeth together. She panted as she crouched there, sighing out.

"I swear," the vampire woman whimpered again. "It was Darcy who contracted us. She set up everything. She said that if Rose was dead, the Sullivans would be weak, and then..." She drifted off into silence, glancing up at Kane.

Kane's long, cold fingers curled into fists, and she slowly lifted her chin.

In that single moment, the woman flicked her gaze up to me, and in that heartbeat, I saw her lip curl, if ever so slightly. That was the only warning we got before she jerked away from Tommie, to the right, a direction that Tommie wasn't expecting, because her grip on the vampire loosened enough for the vampire to roll forward, out of Tommie's grasp. But the vampire woman didn't bolt for the line of trees, away.

She bolted toward *me*.

I didn't know what to do, and it was too quick for me to react or, really, do anything, anyway. I took a quick breath and simply braced myself for impact. I had the presence of mind to let go of Gwen, and she fell to the side, slumping against the ground, but at least out of harm's way. The vampire woman was going to hit me, and we'd roll together, end over end, and we were close enough to the cliff face that I would fall down, down, if I wasn't bitten first. I was going to die.

But I didn't. The woman, close enough for her fingernails to gouge a crescent moon pattern out of my shoulder, was caught out of mid-air by Kane. Kane who moved faster than any living creature was capable of.

And, as I watched, Kane moved her hands from the woman's shoulders up to the woman's head. And in one smooth, fluid motion, Kane twisted the woman's skull in her hands, jerking the neck to the side.

I heard a sickening, wet *snap*, and the woman fell limply at Kane's feet, as boneless as a marionette whose strings are no longer pulled.

She was dead.

"Oh, my God," I whispered, but Kane was at my side then, her cold arm around my waist, still not gazing me in the eyes. She glanced out at sea, and I caught something deep in the depths of her blue gaze. Something I couldn't quite place.

Kane Sullivan, I'd thought, felt no fear.

But she looked afraid, in that heartbeat.

She cleared her throat and glanced down at me and Gwen, shaking her head slightly.

"We must get you inside. It's not safe out here," she growled, and then Tommie was on the other side of me, and she gently took up Gwen in her arms, hefting her up like she weighed nothing, Gwen's limbs and head dangling.

I don't remember much about the climb up the hill. I was in a state of shock, of exhaustion, but I held my own as Kane's tender arm helped steer me and hold me up. We climbed together, slowly, up the rest of the hill, and when we hit the level land of the Sullivan Hotel's parking lot, Kane jerked her chin toward the side door, down to the basement kitchen.

"Gwen's bleeding," she told Tommie tightly, and Tommie nodded once.

The vampires would scent us, I realized with a light head as Kane took us down through the kitchens. Treaty or no treaty, could a vampire control him or herself when there was so much blood?

There was no one at the stove or the counters—they were deserted. There was no one out in the basement hallway or staircase that led up to the front hall.

"Gwen needs a doctor," I told Kane, glancing over at my best friend, at the pallid cast to her face, how slick with sweat her skin was, how brightly colored the blood seemed on her soaked through t-shirt. "We were in an accident," I managed, gripping Kane's arm now. "Her van's totaled. They pushed us off the road."

"I'll take her to the doctor in town," offered Tommie, straightening a little and glancing at me with soft eyes. "You're safe here now, Rose. Stay in my rooms. When I come back, we'll settle this, all right?" Even though she was holding Gwen, she managed to step forward somehow and hold my gaze as her shoulder pressed against mine. "We'll be back soon," she said as she leaned forward, and then her cold lips were pressed against mine.

My heart was roaring through me, and as it

roared, I could feel it tearing in two, right down the middle. Because Tommie's mouth was against mine as Kane's arm was around my waist.

I was held in the middle of two women that I cared about utterly. And, no matter what I did, I was going to hurt them. Perhaps both of them, perhaps one of them. But their pain was inevitable.

As was mine.

Tommie turned on her heel and was down the corridor and out the front door before I could even blink. Gwen would be all right, I knew. I hoped. She had to be. She couldn't be in trouble because of me. She had to be all right.

Kane's jaw worked as she gazed steadily at the floor, at the red and black tiles, and not at me. "Let's get you up to Tommie's rooms, then," she said softly.

And that's when I snapped.

"No," I told her, and I reached up and gripped her shoulder, trying to catch her gaze. I held her violently blue eyes with my own and I swallowed. I was shaking. "I can't do this," I told her. "Everything's not as it should be." I didn't even know what that meant, but it was how I felt, the truest truth inside of me. "Please tell me that you feel it, too."

"What's going on?"

I stiffened, my blood turning to ice in my veins.

Melody.

She was walking down the Widowmaker staircase, the staircase that—on the very first morning of being here—Kane had saved me from. Kane was always saving me, in small ways and big ways, and now here was this woman who had somehow, miraculously, reappeared to take from me that which had never belonged to me…but that which I'd hoped with my whole heart could be mine, if I'd tried hard enough.

I hadn't even been able to try. Melody had taken *everything* from me.

And now she was walking down the steep staircase as if she was a tightrope walker, as if she knew those steps intimately. And she did, I realized. She'd lived in the Sullivan Hotel much, much longer than me.

I took a deep breath and I stepped away from Kane, feeling utterly defeated. Feeling my heart broken and crumbling inside of me, and something that could never, ever be put back together again.

But as I turned to go back down the hallway of paintings, of red and black tile, away from the woman who called to me like a gravity…I was stopped.

Cold, lovely fingers curled around my wrist, holding me in place.

Kane.

When I turned back to look at her, my heart caught in my throat.

Her eyes were soft, as they gazed into mine. The ice blue of them was melted around the edges.

And, as I watched, Kane Sullivan—the strongest woman I'd ever known in my whole life—let a single tear fall from her left eye and traced a path across her perfect cheekbone and skin, drifting down to her chin and falling away into the darkness of the hallway.

"Melody," said Kane then, her low, gravelly voice strong and clear and unwavering. She turned to look at the woman who'd paused on the staircase, the woman who stared at me with shrewd, narrowed eyes, arms crossed, waiting.

We were all waiting. I held my breath. This couldn't possibly be happening.

But then it did.

"Melody, I can't do this anymore. I am so very, very sorry," she said, standing even straighter, glancing up the staircase at the woman who had been her soulmate, the woman she had never forgotten, slipping into sadness over the days, weeks, months and years of a century. The woman she had promised her entire being to. She gazed at this woman, and she breathed out. "I don't know what's happened to you, and I can't fathom the things that you have gone through in the time that we were apart. I'm so sorry you experience that pain and darkness. I did everything I could to keep it from you, and I failed in that. But the connection that we have has been severed. You have become someone cruel and unkind and that is not the woman I knew or loved. The connection that I felt, that I mourned all these years, no longer exists between us. Please forgive me," she said, her voice catching and breaking at the end. "But we can't be together."

Melody's eyes flashed dangerously dark as she turned and glanced down at me now. "Is it because of her?" she asked, her voice chillingly calm. "What has she done to you? What has she told you?" she hissed, descending the last few steps to stand on the level with us, her hands clenched into immoveable fists at her sides. "Did she seduce you?" She drew herself up to her full height, and her words turned utterly imperious. "Have you slept with her?" she asked then, her voice almost a whisper.

"No," said Kane, her voice breaking again. "I would never do anything like that to you, Melody. I have only ever been faithful to you. You and only you. But I do not think we should try to conform something that existed a century ago to something our hearts no longer want. I know," she said, raising her chin and holding Melody's gaze, "that you no longer feel the same way about me that you used to. That you do not want me like you used to. And there is no crime in that, no shame. We did our best to try again, and it was not meant to be. And we must accept that. It's over."

I expected Melody to be upset. Perhaps to say that they needed another chance, that they needed to try again. I could feel Kane wavering as she held tightly to my wrist, as tightly as a drowning woman would grip a lifeline. I knew that she did not want to cause Melody pain. I knew that feeling all too well. If Melody wept at this moment, if she asked for another chance, Kane would grant her that.

But Melody did nothing of the sort.

She tilted her head to the side, her eyes flashing cruelly. "It is not so easy, Kane Sullivan, to break a vow of love. A vow that has lasted over one hundred years. I will not forget this betrayal. And, in time, you will wish you had not done this."

And then in one, fluid motion, she turned and climbed back up the staircase so quickly, that I jumped out of my skin. She contorted her limbs and climbed up the staircase like a spider, dragging her dress after her, the crimson thing flowing upward like blood gone wrong.

In a moment, Melody was gone, but her darkness lingered in the air for a handful of breaths as I stood there, stunned. Melody had just threatened Kane.

…But it didn't matter. Nothing else mattered in that scrap of a moment. Because we stood together, Kane and I.

Kane still held tightly to my wrist, like she was

never going to let it go.

And, it dawned on me as I stared down at her cold fingers wrapped around my skin, that she wouldn't have to, ever again.

Kane had told Melody it was over.

I glanced up into Kane's face, at the war of emotions that raged just beneath the surface of her cold skin. Her eyes were dark, and when they gazed into mine, they didn't see me, not really, not for a long moment.

But then she came back to me. And another tear traced itself down Kane's cheek as she stepped forward quickly, wrapping her hands around my waist, drawing me to her like we were one creature, not two.

When I breathed out into the darkness of that hallway, my breath hung between us like smoke. I inhaled again, inhaling the scent that was Kane, the cigarettes and the jasmine and vanilla and unnamable spice that clung to her cold skin. I stared up into those violently blue eyes, those eyes that held me and only me in that moment. Her gaze was fierce and predatory and wholly mine as she pinned me to the spot with eyes so blue that I drowned in them.

"Forgive me," said Kane, then, and she leaned down gracefully, and in a heartbeat I could never have predicted, her mouth met mine.

# -- Eternal Game --

Kane tasted like fire, a fire that burns like ice. I lifted my chin, kissing her back fiercely, my hands wrapped around the curves of her waist so tightly that—if she wasn't a vampire—I'd be afraid of bruising her.

But this moment didn't seem real. And by gripping her hips, by pressing my fingers hard into her body, into her flesh, I was trying to ground myself in the reality of the situation, of the moment.

Because how could this possibly be happening? Kane was kissing me with such fierceness, such passion, and I'd dreamed of moments like this, yes. But I couldn't have imagined it ever happening to me again.

I didn't want to think anymore. I was done thinking, done worrying, done second-guessing myself, done with dreaming.

I was done with everything but feeling.

And, my God, I was feeling a *lot.*

Kane's hand was at the back of my neck, gently cupped against my skin, her fingers so cold against me as they twined in my hair, as she slowly reached up, drifting her fingers across the nape of my neck, that goosebumps rose along my skin, and I took a deep breath, holding her closer, harder. She touched me like I was something fragile, like this moment between us was something fragile. Like everything could break.

But I'd already broken. I'd already broken into

the smallest pieces when Anna died, and again when Kane said she had feelings for me…and then chose Melody over me. I'd broken, and I'd put myself back together again.

I was done being broken.

I gripped her even harder, tightening my fingers at the curve of her waist beneath her dress shirt. We were standing right by the empty front desk of the Sullivan Hotel, and though there was no one in the entryway or lobby or corridors, this was still hardly a private location. But I didn't care. I'd waited long enough, and that meant that this moment was all I had—so I was going to make the most of it. My body moved on pure instinct alone as I tugged up on her shirt, drawing it out from the waistband of her suit pants, and then my warm fingers were pressed against the cool smoothness of her back, the sculpted lines of her belly.

Someone told me recently that vampires retain the body they had the day they were made into vampires. Branna had told me how hard she and Kane worked back in Ireland, tilling the fields and making a life for their families. Kane's muscles, hard beneath my fingertips, belied an intense hardship and struggle for life, not countless days at the gym.

I kissed Kane, and I reveled in those muscles, tracing circles across them, hooking my fingers into the waistband of her suit pants. The intensity of her kiss brightened just then, quickening, and when I gasped against her, when I drew back a little, I looked up at her wet lips, at her darkened eyes, darkened with hunger, with need, and I knew that she felt everything I did. That she wanted this as much as I did.

Which was more than I'd ever wanted anything

before.

Kane's fingers were wrapped gently around the back of my neck, and I winced a little as her thumb traced over my healing wounds there, right at the curve of my neck and shoulder. They weren't overly large wounds but two deep pinpricks that Mags had given me, only a few days ago. Kane breathed out at my tension, staring down at the wounds, then flicking her gaze up to my eyes, her brow furrowed with worry.

"Does it hurt?" she whispered, her voice low, gruff, as she stroked the pad of her thumb down the side of my neck, away from the hurt. I shivered beneath her touch, the entire focus of my being in her fingertips and where those fingertips met my skin.

"Only a little," I told her truthfully, then reached up, placing my hand on top of hers, and pressing her hand down against my skin so that her cool palm went flat upon me. She put her head to the side, watching me closely. "It's nothing to worry about... It's well on its way to being healed." I licked my lips, shifted my weight back into my heels; then I reached up and wrapped my arms tightly around her neck, pulling her down to me so that our foreheads brushed against one another, so that she closed her eyes, breathing out, her nostrils flaring, as she slowly, gently, breathed me in. "It...it doesn't matter," is what I whispered to her then, my voice strained, breaking on the last few words. I took a deep breath, I stared up into her bright blue eyes, and I whispered to her the truth. My truth. "I need you."

Kane stiffened beneath my hands, and her already dark eyes gazed down into mine with such bright ferocity in that moment that I was undone by it. Her breathing was already fast, but when her beautiful, wet mouth parted then, when she breathed out, when she drew me to her with such strength, so that the front of my body was pressed hard against her, I lost any last semblance of self control I'd heaped upon myself these past few days working at the Sullivan Hotel.

I gripped her hips roughly, I curled my fingers at the back of her neck, and I drew her down to me for a wild kiss. And then I repeated it, the truth, breathing it out into the stillness between us. "*I need you,*" I told her, my voice a low growl. "I need you *right now.*"

I'd waited patiently. I'd believed that it was over between us, the blossoming, unfurling thing that we'd started one night on the beach... Had it only been a few days ago? It felt like a lifetime had already passed since that first kiss, my heels sinking into the sand, her hands gentle on my hips as she drew me to her gently—again, as if I could break. But, again, I'd already been broken. I'd dealt with my broken heart, and I'd moved on, or at least I kidded myself into believing I had, after that night. But it was impossible, "moving on."

Because it was always Kane for me. It had always been Kane, always would be Kane. I had never been drawn to anyone or anything like her in my entire life, and I'd never known it could be like this. That I could *feel* the connection between us, unfurling like light, a string I could actually feel wrapped around my heart snugly, connected to hers. No matter how far apart we were, I felt it.

No matter how far apart we were, I felt *her.*

Kane's breathing was ragged as she glanced up, past me, down the corridor of paintings in front of us that led away from the front desk and the entrance to the Sullivan Hotel. She seemed to be weighing something in her head, because she also glanced at one of the leather couches in the entryway, as if that might be the best option. But she appeared to make up her mind then.

"Come on," she said, and her voice was still gruff as she threaded my arm through hers, turning and starting down the corridor of paintings, toward the eventual staircase at the end of it.

Though Kane's legs were longer than mine, I didn't struggle to keep up. I actually set the pace, pulling her along, glancing over my shoulder with my heart in my throat, my heart that was pumping blood through me at a speed that should probably make me dead. When I glanced back at Kane, I saw the darkness in her eyes. I saw the corners of her mouth turn up, just slightly, but it was almost impossible to tell what she was thinking. She'd gone internal, like she was thinking about something, weighing something heavily, and I didn't want her to think anymore, either.

We'd done enough thinking, enough rationalizing, for an entire lifetime.

We both needed to feel now. Feel each other. Come down from our heads and hearts into our bodies, and experience each other on a purely physical level.

I pulled her up the staircase, moving quickly, and she was right behind me. I could hear her breathing, could hear the movement of her clothing against her skin, the soft *shush* of her white-gold hair falling over her shoulder and behind her, down her back like a waterfall. I could feel her other hand at the inward curve of my waist, at my hip…even against my ass as she touched me as we moved. They were light touches, her fingers brushing against me in something you could almost think of as an accident. But her movements were not accidental, and when we got to the floor where the Sullivans had their bedrooms, she pulled me up, stopping me.

I turned, wondering, but I didn't get a chance to ask her anything, because she watched me carefully, her eyes narrowed, as she curled her fingers at my hips and she pressed me up against the wall beside the staircase landing. She gripped me fiercely, her hips pressing against my own with her full weight, and when she bent her beautiful head, her hair falling over her shoulder again as her mouth fit itself at the curve of my jaw and neck, she kissed me so fiercely there that—for a heartbeat—I kind of wondered if she was going to bite me.

This being with a vampire thing…it was kind of new. Sexy, definitely. God, *definitely*. But, also, there was the constant knowledge in the back of my head that the woman who was drawing her mouth in a cold, searing trail of kisses down my neck had teeth that could puncture my skin without a moment's warning. Her teeth were so sharp, in fact, that I might not even feel it until afterward, the slices in my skin leaking blood, and her mouth there, drinking me up, her tongue laving my neck as she swallowed it down.

But here's the thing about Kane: I trusted her. I trusted her with my very life. Hadn't she just saved my life, saved my life multiple times in the days I'd lived here at the Sullivan Hotel? Yes, I trusted her. I trusted her enough that I tilted my head back against the wall, exposing more of my neck to her, closing my eyes as she traced her cool tongue across my skin, shuddering a little against her palms as she pressed my hips harder against the wall. I could feel the fabric of my skirt inching up my thighs, and we were right out there in the corridor, and it was only early evening. Anyone could have come by at that moment as I wrapped my arms around her neck, urging her to be harder, quicker…less delicate.

Yes, I wanted her. I wanted her so deeply, so profoundly, that my entire body pulsed with that want, moving through me quicker than blood.

"Come," she murmured then, her mouth against my skin as she breathed that single word, growling it against my body like an invitation. She straightened, standing, her eyes so dark that they were almost black as she gazed down into my face, her mouth open, parted, her breath coming even faster, as she practically panted, trying to compose herself. But there was no time for that. She pushed off from the wall and bit her lip as she tugged on my hand, pulling me after her, and leading me, now, down the wide corridor. The floor beneath us was the black-and-red tile, so signature of the Sullivan Hotel, and along the two walls stretching out on either side of us stood the tall, ornamented wooden doors that led to the bedrooms of the vampires.

As we passed by Tommie's door, a small, silver plaque beside the door bearing the inscription in cursive, "T. Sullivan," I gave a little involuntary shiver. I'd stayed there just last night, in Tommie's arms. Just last night, I'd felt Tommie's fingers against my skin… I took a deep breath as we passed by the door, and I couldn't help wondering where was Tommie right then. Gwen had been hurt in the accident—was it a mere hour ago now?—and Tommie had volunteered to take her to the doctor in town, because Tommie was wonderful like that. Tommie had told me to wait in her room for her, that I'd be safe there after everything that had happened, after the two vampires had tried to kill both Gwen and me... But here and now, it was Kane who was leading me down the corridor, leading me past Tommie's room, continuing on, her hand confident and cold in my own as she gripped me tightly.

I couldn't help it. At that moment, when I blinked, I saw Anna, holding me and touching me, kissing me and smiling at me. When I closed my eyes, I saw Tommie's bright green eyes, her sly smile and her hopeful voice. My heart ached for a long moment, and it was only right. It had been a long time since Anna, but she was still a part of me, would always be a part of me. And Tommie... She'd helped me when I'd had no one else. There would always be a part of my heart, even if it was a small part, that cared for her fiercely.

But those thoughts came into my head and heart, and then they slowly eased out of me, the tension draining from me, my past pain felt and heard...and now no longer required. It was just Kane and me in the hallway, and the shadows of sadness and ache inside of me would always remain.

But I didn't need to feel them right now.

So my heart ached, but in the few heartbeats I had between Tommie's door and Kane's, the latter one being just as tall and ornamented and imposing as the others, with a little plaque beside it elegantly reading "K. Sullivan," I knew I had to push all thoughts of Tommie out of my head and heart. We had gone on a few dates these past days, but we weren't dating, the two of us. Not yet.

It was a cowardly distinction, and there was going to be hell to pay because of this, and I was going to cause Tommie immense pain, just as I knew I would... I'd known that, somehow, someway, someone was going to get hurt because of all of this.

But right there and then, after wanting so much, after being hurt so much, after fixing my own broken heart and rising again…there was nothing I wanted more than Kane Sullivan.

Come what may.

Kane and I walked together, side by side, hands clasped dearly, until we reached Kane's door. She paused in front of it, not looking at the impressive wooden thing but glancing back at me as she reached out toward the door. It opened beneath the touch of her hand. I guess vampires probably really never felt the need to lock their doors.

We stepped over the threshold, Kane and I, and then I simply glanced at her. She'd dropped my hand once we were in her room, and she had her hands at her suit jacket collar, straightening it…but then my hands were covering her own, and I was pushing Kane against the wall beside the door while I clumsily toed the door shut, the thing banging hard, sending a reverberation throughout the quiet floor.

We were finally, blessedly, alone. Just the two of us.

My mouth was at her throat, kissing the chill skin there, my hands at the lapel of her jacket, pushing it down around her shoulders, pulling it off of her. It fell into an unceremonious heap beside us on the floor, but I was no longer paying attention to the discarded garment—my fingers were at the top button of her dress shirt, pulling the fine tie loose from its tight knot at her neck.

Kane's mouth was open, and she was breathing quickly, her pupils dilated, her irises—usually so blue, so bright—were dark enough that I was beginning to wonder if the irises had disappeared entirely, or if they were really black now. There was a little light in the room, though what it was coming from I wasn't certain (and I wasn't really interested in her decorating tastes at the moment), but there was enough light to see that Kane's eyes had changed completely.

A thrill ran through me as I pulled the knot of her tie loose, pulling the tie completely undone. The satin fabric slid like water beneath my fingers as I left it hanging, undone and open, around her neck, and then watching her carefully, I reached up my fingers to her stiff collar, touching that first fine button. And then I undid it, shivering against her. My hips were pressed tightly against her own, my fingers shaking a little as the shiver moved through me—but then she was reaching up, covering my hands…and pausing them.

I glanced up at her, worried I'd done something wrong, worried that the moment had come and gone, and that somehow, impossibly, every good thing that had just happened these last few moments had been reversed. I couldn't have predicted this, any of this, so I certainly couldn't predict what would happen next.

But there was nothing dire. There was no Melody opening the door, stopping us. There was nothing that stood between Kane and me except a little bit of clothing.

Kane cleared her throat, shook her head a little. "Would you like a drink?" she asked me then, her voice low and dark and wanting.

"No," I told her then, and I meant it. She stared down at me in surprise, but I was already shaking my head. "I don't want a drink," I whispered to her, threading my fingers through hers. She held my hands tightly over her heart and that first beautiful undone button of her shirt. "I don't want anything but you," I whispered.

Kane's eyes glittered for a moment, and then her jaw tightened, and she nodded, only once, as she bent her face toward me. Kane traced her hands down my back, then, down over my hips, my ass, and to my thighs. She wrapped her fingers tightly around my thighs, and she lifted. One smooth motion up, lifting me like I was practically weightless (vampires, I was beginning to understand, were *really* strong), and I was straddling her, my center pressing tightly against her hips, my legs tightly wrapped around her waist, my arms around her neck and shoulders.

"Please," she whispered then, her voice husky, broken, as she held my gaze. "I need to touch you." Her fingers stroked the backs of my thighs as she held me there against her.

"Yes," I told her, a syllable spoken by my entire body as she carried me into the room, to the big, four-poster bed in the very center of it. "Yes," I repeated as she bent forward, as she lay me down softly, gently, on top of the plush, night-black duvet. "Yes," I whispered into the half-light as Kane stood over me then, peeling off the suspenders from her shoulders as she stared down at me with hooded eyes. Yes, she was actually wearing black suspenders, an exquisite detail I would never forget. The suspenders slipped from her fingers and fell, still attached to her suit pants but now dangling around her thighs.

Kane knelt down onto the bed then, crouching there between my legs as she placed one hand on either side of my waist as I reached up for her. And I did that which I'd always wanted to do: I took her ponytail holder, a thin elastic band, and I pulled it out.

It was surreal and lovely, how her white-gold mane fell around the both of us. She had such long white-blonde hair that it seemed to drape around the both of us, obscuring everything but her and me in that moment. I reached up, and I ran my fingers through thin, satiny strands, and I felt the coolness of her hair against my palms as I arched beneath her, drawing her down to me. And Kane descended, descended like a fallen angel, to capture my mouth with hers.

I was wearing a knee-length skirt and blouse, but because it was a remarkably warm day, I hadn't felt the need to wear tights or leggings with the skirt. So when Kane slid her cold, soft hands up my right calf, I gasped against her. She was so chill to the touch, and touching me didn't warm her skin at all. But it was perfect, how her wintry skin felt against the heat of my own; teasing, how chill her palm felt as she traced her long fingers up to the curve of my knee, to the soft skin behind my knee, and then down, down to my thigh as she placed her hand full against me, drawing a gasp of pleasure from me as I arched beneath her, desperate for my center to, once more, feel that connection to her.

Kane stared down into my eyes as I reached up to wrap my arms around her neck again. I drew her down to me, pulled her to me like a ship drawing in its anchor, and when her mouth connected with mine, I finally understood how cold can be hot.

Because Kane's mouth was searingly chill against my skin, her tongue cold against my tongue—but she was so cold that it seemed that her body had looped back around to hot again, as she pressed her palm against my stomach, having inched up the hem of my shirt from the waistband of my skirt. She raked her short nails across my skin, and I hissed out against her, my eyes rolling back, my head and neck arching as I lifted my chest to her, asking with my body.

And she answered.

Kane tugged up my shirt all the way, until she pulled it off of me, over my head and tossed it aside, and then Kane's fingers were at the edge of my right bra cup and the lace there, tracing a finger over the soft lace for half a moment while she watched her fingers against the cloth and my skin, her eyes dark and feverish with something I felt just as fiercely. I ached for more than this, and she seemed to know it, knowing not to tease me, because she couldn't bear the tease either as she pulled my bra cup down to expose my breast to the cool air, and her cooler mouth.

"Ah," I whispered, biting my lip—hard—as she bit my nipple. It's as if she'd been chewing peppermint gum, or had just eaten an ice cube, her mouth was that cold, and instantly both of my nipples were peaked, one in her mouth, aching from her attentions, and the other straining and aching against my other bra cup. But, as she kissed my right breast, she pulled down the other cup and flicked her thumbnail against my hard nipple, eliciting another gasp from me.

My bra straps were pulled down my shoulders then, falling around my arms, as she bent over me, her soft, white-gold hair trailing over my skin, making me shiver against her. Kane moved, only a little, and then her right knee was at my center, while she continued to tease and lick and nip my breasts, pinching my nipples with her fingers, biting down with just enough pressure that it hurt just right, just right to be so pleasurable that my eyes were rolling back in my head as I arched up beneath her, seeking some sort of release.

And I found it when her knee moved against

my center. I still wore my panties, she still wore her pants, but the friction felt so good. Not enough, never enough, but a start, and I gripped her hips so tightly with my hands, grinding down on her leg, that I was panting as she remained above me, her mouth cool against my heart.

When Kane rose above me again, raking her fingers through her hair so that it settled around her shoulders, I looked up at her, breathing out into the half-light as I paused. She'd…changed.

Her irises, if they had been dark before…they were fully black now. And her incisors were…well, pointy.

"Kane?" I whispered, still panting as I reached up, undoing the bottom few buttons of her shirt. I slipped my fingers against her muscled belly, and I traced my fingers over those muscles uncertainly. "Are you…are you okay?" I asked her, biting my lip as I stared up at her, watching her.

"Yes," she whispered, and she crouched over me, her brow furrowing. "I'm sorry…" She closed her mouth and ran her tongue over her front teeth. "This is what happens when we're…aroused." She licked her lips, her jaw tightening. "Do I frighten you?" she asked me, her voice low and longing…and sad. She opened her mouth to breathe out, and her sharp incisors glittered in the low light.

"No," I whispered, before she'd even been able to complete the question. Yes, Kane was a vampire—but there was nothing about her that I didn't trust, that I wasn't enthralled with, that I didn't feel connected to with every part of my body and heart. It's hard to put into words even now, even after all these years, as I consider that moment and my reaction to that question.

It's as if she'd asked me if I could breathe water. No. Of course not. Of course she didn't frighten me. Everything that I was, every cell and atom and quark inside of me was drawn to her. I knew her, knew her heart, and I didn't know how I knew. But I did.

And I knew that she loved me. Even then, I knew.

And I loved her, too.

"No," I repeated, shaking my head as I wrapped my arms around her neck, drawing her down to me. She stared down at me with dark eyes as I held her gaze, as I brushed a stray strand of white-blonde hair behind her ear, staring up at her beauty, at her face that I'd dreamed of, every night since coming to the Sullivan Hotel. Her face that I somehow, impossibly, remembered. "You don't frighten me." I licked my lips, too, and then I arched my head back against the duvet, exposing my bare neck to her…asking for a kiss.

And she bent her graceful head down to me, placing her full lips against the skin of my throat. And she kissed me there, one soft, cold kiss, and she kissed me again, her mouth open, her tongue laving my skin. She kissed me again, and she bit me, but very softly, her sharp incisors brushing against me with great gentleness, her fingers tender now, as she gripped me tightly, then less tender, fiercer, her fingers, even with their short nails, sharp against my skin.

I pressed against her thigh, and I bucked my hips, panting out against her. Her breath was cold on my skin as she breathed out, placing one last, gentle kiss against the thrumming vein in my neck. And she rose, glancing up at me again, her dark eyes flickering.

Kane was straddling me, arching over me, as she traced a line down the front of my body, over my right breast and the bra, still around my middle, down my stomach and over the fabric of my skirt, down to my hips and right thigh. I shivered against her as she paused, trailing her fingertips back up my thigh, over my hot skin, to press against the front of my panties.

She watched me, locking her gaze with mine, as her thumb pressed down onto my center, the heel of her hand hard against my clit. I shuddered against her, but I kept her gaze, too. There was something about gripping her shoulders tightly, my fingernails marking her skin, surely. Something about holding that gaze. Her eyes were dark, but in their darkness, they seemed even more alive; they flashed with an inner fire that pierced me through. Her eyes saw to the very depths of me, as her fingers traced patterns over my center, going back and forth, back and forth, gently, almost delicately, but enough that a hiss of desire escaped my lips, and I pressed down onto her hand with my own, asking with my body, asking again. Please.

I must have said it out loud, because something moved across her face…and if I thought she wanted me before now... Well. I didn't know how much she could want me. Because Kane sat back on her heels, and in one effortless motion, she took the waistband of my panties and pulled them smoothly off of me, down my hips and legs. She tossed them over her shoulder, and her mouth was at my right knee now, kissing me gently, breathing out against my skin as she closed her eyes; her dark lashes fluttered against her pale cheeks as she breathed out into the stillness, inhaling the scent of me.

"Please," I whispered, then. She looked at me instantly, her dark eyes flashing, and I gripped her shoulder hard, leaving little half-moons in her skin, my nails holding tight to her. "Please," I repeated, shaking my head, licking my lips. "I can't wait anymore."

"Neither can I," said Kane, and she shook her head, pushing off the bed and up, standing at the edge of it, then. I rose to my elbows, and I watched her, watched her carefully and quickly unbutton every button on her shirt. I watched that shirt fall from her creamy shoulders, down to the floor, watched her as she raked her fingers through her hair, to the side, so that the white-gold, shimmering strands fell, cascading over her bare right arm, and down. I watched her undo the button and zipper on her suit pants, watched her remove them with a single motion, watched them fall to the floor with her boyshorts. The shoes were gone in a moment, and then Kane stood there, stood there with her long, lean body that seemed so pale in the half-light. She wore a single metal cuff on her wrist, a wide, thick bit of metal I hadn't noticed before—it was covered in Irish symbols. A triskel, though I didn't know that word at the time, was front and center on the wide cuff.

But, let's be honest…my eyes weren't lingering on her singular piece of jewelry.

This was the first time that I'd seen Kane's body, and as my heart rose into my throat, as she stood there for only a heartbeat longer before she descended to me again…that moment, that heartbeat, will linger in my memory for eternity.

Kane was tall, taller than me by about a head, and her legs were long and lean—I knew these things about her body already. My fingertips had already traced the muscled contours of her belly, so I knew she was muscled, too, but it was hard to discern how muscled she was beneath the men's suits she always wore, the tie drawn up around her neck, the dress shirt always buttoned to its topmost button.

Now, here, devoid of all of that, my eyes traced her lines and curves, her muscled belly and her muscled thighs, the rise and fall and curve of her hips, the perfect shape of her breasts. Her nipples were startlingly pink—I think "startling," because the rest of her was so pale, ashen and milk-white. The curve of her breasts was small, but high and round. Vampires retain the body they had when they were bitten. Here and now, I saw the hard work Kane must have endured in Ireland, hundreds of years ago. I couldn't imagine her life then, what she must have seen and done, trying to carry the weight of a farm on her shoulders, the weight of her family's welfare.

But I didn't see just sadness, though I knew the stories of her muscles, of strong hands and thighs and arms, was one of sadness.

I also saw beauty, beauty vast and deep, not because it was conventional, but because she was so beautiful to *me*. Because she *was*. Every line and every curve of her called to me, begged for me to touch and kiss and worship. I wanted to put my mouth in every bend of her, breathe in every inch of her skin, kiss it and caress it and mark it as mine with tongue and teeth and touch. The waterfall of her mane cascaded down her back, over her well-muscled shoulders, and as she stood there with her feet apart, her arms easy at her sides, her chin lifted and her eyes glittering in the dark, I could feel the pull between us, the line from my heart to hers…tightening.

"Come here," I told her, my voice low, shaking, as I lifted a hand to her, holding it out, palm up.

And she came.

Kane knelt down on the edge of the bed, knelt

down between my legs. On her hands and knees, and yet still so very, very powerful, she arched over me, her dark eyes glittering with need for a long moment before she closed her eyes. Her long lashes lay against her pale cheeks, and then she bent her beautiful head, and she breathed out into my palm, placing a delicate, haunting kiss there, against my skin.

I licked my lips, my heart about to beat itself out of my chest. I still held myself up with one elbow beneath me, and now I turned my head to the side. I licked my lips. I tried to still my erratically beating heart (and failed).

"Closer," I whispered to her.

Kane's mouth turned up deliciously at the corners, and there was mischief there as she rose off her heels, curving her body over mine now, her right arm holding her up, her hand positioned beside my waist, but her other arm was looping beneath my waist, then going under my body. Kane sat back on her heels again as she lifted me up, and I was surprised at how strong she was, because I think there were some moments where I was still forgetting exactly what she was, where I was still expecting her to act human, be human. But Kane was not human, and had not been human for a very long time.

Kane lifted me into her lap as she turned around smoothly, moving herself to the center of the bed, and she sat there, cross-legged, with my own legs wrapped around her waist, her arms wrapped around me tightly and holding me to her like she was never going to let go while I straddled her, sitting in her lap.

Kane kissed me then, while we were heart to heart. Her cold skin against my own made me shiver with delight as she kissed me long and deep, her tongue raking through my mouth with need. She was aware of her pointed incisors and was gentle, letting me set the pace, and we moved together in that kiss, every part of me aching.

My center was not quite pressed against her pelvis, and that's what I wanted, and I ground down a little onto her lap as she traced a hand down my back, raking her short fingernails over me to cup her hand on my ass, holding me in place and bringing me a little snugger against her. She traced those fingers over my hip and thigh, and then she was dipping her hand between us.

There was absolutely nothing that stood between Kane and me anymore, and when her fingers turned and then gently brushed against my opening, I breathed out, moaning into the darkness, because I'd never wanted anything more than I wanted her in that moment. And Kane knew it—she felt my want, radiating off of my body like light, and she bent her head, tracing her tongue over my chest until she captured my left nipple with her mouth. And when she did that, when she bit down gently, her sharp incisors drifting over my skin with delicacy…that's when she entered me.

Kane was so cold at first, her fingers ice cold, and it was shocking and delicious all at once as she curved her fingers into me, brushing her thumb over my clit, pressing down with the heel of her hand and moving her hips, using them as leverage for her hand so that her fingers pushed in deeper.

Kane touched me, watching me with her darkened eyes, her mouth open, parted, as she panted against me, as she moved her hips, pushing her hand back and forth, making her fingers come and go, entering me deeply and almost leaving me…but not quite. The rhythm was exactly what I needed, and it grounded me in that moment, that moment with her.

My arms were wrapped around her, and her left arm was wrapped around me. We were as close as two creatures could possibly get, wrapped up in one another, our limbs contorted and tangled, our hearts pressed tightly together. I cried out, threading my fingers through her hair, tightly against her scalp, pulling and twisting as I flung my head back, as I pulsed my hips up and down onto her hand. I knew what felt good, and so did she, and she was drawing this exquisite pleasure from me, as if she'd done this hundreds of times before. As if she knew exactly what it took to bring me to the edge of ecstasy, and then over it.

Kane kissed my neck softly, slowly, my shoulder, cold kisses that made me shiver against her, crying out again, as I pushed myself down on her hand, craving release. It was when I drew her face to mine, when I kissed her again, hard, fiercely, feeling her cold mouth against mine, her fingers inside of me, her thumb against my clit, her entire body wrapped tightly with mine…that's when I came.

It was sudden and immediate and surprising, the orgasm that raked through me. Kane hissed out against me in pleasure as she felt my muscles contract against her fingers, as she felt my wetness coat her hand. She slowed down the rhythm, and she coaxed me longer, higher, until my eyelashes fluttered against my cheeks, until every muscle in my entire body was softly shivering with pleasure. Then she pulled her wet fingers from me, lying back down upon the pillows, drawing me with her. I lay on top of her, my entire body trembling, my breathing still coming fast, and she wrapped her arms tightly around me, embracing me so tenderly that I felt fully held.

Pleasure still radiated, like a shooting star, through every atom of me as I straightened up, rising over her, still straddling her. I placed my hands onto her muscled stomach, and I stared down at Kane, one arm pillowed beneath her head, a soft smile turning up the corners of her mouth so beautifully that my still-thrumming heart skipped a beat. Her eyes were still darkened, her incisors were still fanged, and as I looked down at this beautiful vampire, this beautiful vampire that I knew I loved, loved deeply, madly, truly, I wanted nothing more than to make her feel just as good as she'd made me feel.

I glanced down, and I watched my fingers as they traced the contours of her belly, drawing soft patterns as I trailed my fingertips up and over her skin, up to her breasts. Her nipples were hard against my fingers as I brushed over them with my hot skin. Her cold and my heat together made for a decadent combination, and Kane's eyelashes fluttered before she closed her eyes, opened her mouth—breathed out into the stillness.

I still straddled her hips, and her skin was slick beneath my center. I trailed my first finger down, down, over her, until it was beneath me. I moved through my own wetness, dragging some down with my fingertips, until my hand was entirely between us, and my fingers were at her center.

God, she was so wet. I flushed when I felt her wetness, flushed with desire that I didn't even know I had in me, it was so powerful, so complete. I moved off of her, to the side, and I lay down beside her, my full length against her, putting my weight on my left elbow as I leaned over her, gazing down at her beautiful face, her beautiful body, every inch of her muscled, milk-white skin something that called to me like we'd done this so many times before.

But we…hadn't. This was our very first time, the moment I'd been waiting for subconsciously (and also very much consciously) since I'd first met Kane Sullivan. We had never been together before tonight. But as I trailed my fingertips down over her belly again, as she spread her legs for me, drawing her right leg up and over my hips to open herself as much as she could to me, I drew my fingers over her wetness, and I was shocked at how familiar a sensation this was, this touch, this sweetness on my fingers, her body already asking beneath my hand as her hips began to move in a rhythm, even before I began earnestly touching her.

Maybe it was because of Anna, I thought, as I brushed my fingertips over her center again. I was teasing Kane, I knew, and she moaned a little, her hand going quickly to my wrist as she stared up at me, her jaw clenched. She pushed my hand down, over her center insistently, but I drew my fingers over her lightly again, like I was playing an instrument, and I was just plucking the first few chords to warm up.

Why did this seem so familiar? Yes, Anna and I had moved like this, me on my elbow beside her, her leg thrown over my body to allow my hand whatever it wanted, opening herself fully to me. We'd moved together just like this…but it wasn't the familiarity or pain of Anna that I thought of when I stared down at Kane.

Have you ever gotten déjà vu so pronounced, so powerful, that you had to stand still for a long moment, your heart thundering inside of you as you wonder what the hell that could possibly have been, that feeling that you had already been here, done this, whatever "this" was, before? I had gotten déjà vu so many times in my life, so many times, and it was an almost uncomfortable feeling, it was so powerful.

But at that moment, it wasn't uncomfortable at all. It was just...weird.

And it was the most powerful déjà vu I'd ever felt.

"Rose?" Kane whispered, and I started, glancing down at her as I fully came back to the moment.

"I'm sorry," I whispered, giving her a soft smile as I lay my hand against her belly. "I just...I was just... This feels a little weird, don't you think?" She stared up at me, her brows furrowing, and I shook my head quickly. "*Good* weird," I told her, my words coming fast. "But doesn't it seem like we've done this before? Kinda like déjà vu a little."

Kane's eyes burned deeply into mine. "I feel it, too," she admitted, her voice low. "Like we've done this before. But we haven't, obviously," she said with a soft chuckle. But her eyes told me that she wasn't so sure.

"Maybe," I told her, getting up and moving slowly, prowling on my hands and knees to crouch between her legs. I gave her a mischievous smile now, glancing up at her as I put my head to the side. "Maybe we met each other in our dreams before. I know I've dreamed about you a lot."

Kane gazed up at me, her arm still pillowed beneath her head, her breasts rising and falling as her breath quickened. "I have dreamed of you, too," she told me, her voice soft and full of longing. "I have dreamed of you so much."

"You have?" I asked her, placing my hands on her knees, tracing my fingers over her thighs. I paused for a moment, surprised. "What have you dreamed about?" I whispered.

"This moment," she said, her eyes narrowed as she considered her words thoughtfully. "Your soft, red hair against my thigh," she said, her voice low, growling. I placed a kiss against her thigh, and then I pillowed my cheek there, staring up at her, my heart thundering through every part of me as desire flooded my cells. She breathed out, licked her lips and spread her legs a little wider as she reached for me with her other hand. I took her hand, and I kissed its palm, its knuckles…each finger, smelling my scent on her skin and feeling desire roar through me like lightning now, too quick, too insistent.

I needed her.

"I dreamed of your mouth," she whispered, her voice thick with need. "I dreamed of your tongue."

I glanced one last time into her beautiful, black eyes. I memorized the way her mouth was open, her full lips wet, her chest rising and falling in the stillness quickly as she reached for me, threading her fingers through my hair. I laid down on my belly, pressing kisses to the extraordinarily soft skin of her thighs, inhaling the scent of her, the sweet, perfumed scent of her skin, of the jasmine and spice merging with the scent of her wetness. All of it came together, spiraling into an aroma that made my entire body come alive. I lowered my mouth to her glistening center. I inhaled deeply. And I kissed her there.

It started as a soft kiss, close-mouthed, tender…and then my mouth opened, and my tongue entered her folds in one first, curious exploration. I tasted her on my tongue, and my eyes rolled back a little, and my breathing quickened, and I sighed out against her, causing her fingers to tighten in my hair, twisting strands around each finger so that her hand was as close to my scalp as she could get.

She tasted like perfection, a sweet muskiness that was cold, like snow, melting on the tongue, and precious, like a lick of a silver spoon, the sweet tang of metal somehow merging with the crisp cold. She tasted like these things, yes, but she also tasted like…well, like Kane.

And I knew I'd tasted her before.

It was impossible, of course. Of course I'd never been here, lying between her legs like a worshipful supplicant, tasting a divine being, her fingers in my hair. But I felt like I *had*, and that's what made me pause for a moment, tasting her for that first time, breathing in her scent, feeling the softness of her thighs beneath my hands, her wetness on my nose, my mouth, my chin. It was all so familiar, and in its familiarity, it was disconcerting.

But Kane's fingers threaded through my hair a little deeper, pushing my face gently against her, urging me, asking me with her hands, with her faster breathing, with her soft, deep moan that was meant for me and only me. Kane brought me back to the moment, and in the moment I stayed as I inhaled her again, lifting my chin and tasting her once more. The déjà vu feeling faded away as I lapped at her center, drawing her wetness back up to her clit.

When my tongue touched her clit that first time, a spasm raked through her body. She hadn't told me if vampire bodies were any different from human bodies, apart from the fact that their incisors lengthened and their eyes darkened when they were aroused. I didn't know what to expect, or how, exactly, to bring her to orgasm (I was assuming that this was something vampires could do, too, but what if I was wrong?), but I went into it with my whole heart, wanting to feel her muscles contract, wanting to feel her hands tighten in my hair. I wanted to hear her cry out my name, and I wanted to make her feel as good as she'd made me feel.

So I teased her, and I touched her; I tasted her, and I drew out of her moans and hisses into the half-light as she tightened her grip in my hair, as she pushed my head down against her mound, as she whispered my name into the stillness between us. All we were, in those moments, was a tangle of two bodies, learning the slopes and curves of each other, and all I was seemed to disappear as we merged, Kane and I.

And then she did cry out my name, her fingers so tight in my hair that I sighed as she came, her fingers wound up in my wavy tangles, my fingers deep inside of her, my mouth kissing her and tempting her, and drawing out of her a voice I'd never heard before. It was deep and dark and a low, perfect growl, as she whispered that single syllable into the air:

"Rose," she said, and she whispered it again, her entire body shaking, arching beneath me, as I kept going, as I urged more and more pleasure out of her until her thighs quivered against my ears, and she tugged on my hair, pulling me up. And I came up, then, crawling on top of her to lie out my length over hers. She wrapped her arms tightly around me, and we stayed like that until I started to shiver—not from pleasure, but because I was so cold. The room was chill, and she was chill, too, so I tugged on the duvet and pulled it on top of us, covering us both. And in that tight cocoon, my body heat began to warm Kane. And her body took on my heat and became almost like mine—warm to the touch.

Almost human.

Kane kissed my face, tasting herself on me as she smiled against my mouth. When she pulled back, when she gazed up at me, there was such softness to her features. Like she was, for the first time since I'd known her, well and truly happy.

And that, above all other things, filled my heart with a searing joy.

Joy. I remembered that emotion, but I hadn't felt it over half a year. And I'd never felt joy like this. It was as if light itself had moved through my bloodstream, filling every part of me with something that glimmered, like gold. I stared down at her, and I brushed the pad of my thumb over her high cheekbone, over her jawline, over her full lips. She stared up at me, her black eyes slowly, as I watched, becoming blue again, the blue blossoming up in the darkness like light on the surface of the sea, seen from far, far below.

Like the light of the sun, seen by a drowning man.

"Rose," Kane whispered, moving her lips against my thumb softly, slowly, and I straightened a little, gazing down at her.

"Yes," I told her, not a question. I loved, so much, when she spoke my name, but I loved it even more when we were heart to heart, when she was naked against me, when our bodies were entwined so I wasn't sure where I began or she ended, or if we were still merged.

"I love you," Kane told me then.

They were quiet, those three words that came from her mouth, low and still. There was no preamble, no big buildup. She'd been silent one moment, and then into the silence between us, those three words were born.

I stared down at her, feeling my heart thrum against my bones, feeling the heat of my body warm hers, too, and I *felt* the depth of those words, felt the strength and power of them as I breathed out, as she held me close.

For a long moment, I couldn't speak, I was so overcome. With emotion, with completion…with love. Because I had been falling in love with Kane Sullivan from the very first moment I walked through the enormous front doors of the Sullivan Hotel. My life had seemed, for so long, to be harsh and hard and unlivable. For so long, I'd been going through each day with a hopelessness so profound that I'd felt completely empty.

But I no longer felt empty. Right then and there, I felt so full of love that the emptiness began to fill up with something beautiful.

Love is a seed, and from that seed, once planted, anything can grow. I knew, in that moment, that no matter what happened between Kane and me, love had changed me.

I was changed for good.

I blinked back tears, and I touched her face gently, cupping it in both my hands. "I love you, too," I told her then, and my voice caught on the ends of those words, but they were the truth. The truth that ran through every inch of me, the truth that felt as vibrant and bright and white-hot as a star.

Had I only known Kane for a few days? Yes.

Yes, it had just been a few days. But it *felt* like a lifetime, like I'd known her laughter, her smile, her touch, her hands, her kiss, for so much longer than a few days.

Could love grow in a few days? Did it matter? I didn't know if it was possible, but I knew that, for myself, that's exactly what had happened.

From the very first moment that I'd met Kane Sullivan, I had been drawn to her inexorably. And now, the two of us were together.

And it was the most natural, obvious, wonderful thing in this or any other world. My entire life, I had been moving, always, toward Kane. I'd never known it until that moment. We would have been drawn together if we'd been on opposite sides of the globe. No matter when, no matter how, I would always find her.

We were meant to be.

I knew it might be difficult, going forward. I knew that the world was going to be a difficult place to live in. I knew that Melody had threatened Kane; I knew that I was going to hurt Tommie with this... There were so many hard things ahead of us.

But, right here and now, I lay down on top of Kane, felt her arms tighten around me, lay my head upon her heart, and I listened to the slow, steady beat, a rhythm that was so soothing and lovely to me that I was soon fast asleep.

I loved Kane Sullivan with my whole heart. And no matter what happened after, in that moment, I knew perfect happiness.

And I dreamed.

I was in Kane's arms, in bed with her, and it was the same bed, with the same oaken pillars at the corners of the mattress, the same room. Though I hadn't had a chance to see much of it earlier, I knew it was the same room. But things were different from before. Off. I was wearing something filmy and gauzy and positively see-through, and Kane wore a man's suit, but it was different, too. Older, somehow, with lace at her sleeves, and coattails.

Her outfit looked a little Victorian.

"Wake up, my love," Kane told me teasingly, and when I glanced up at her face, I was surprised. I'd seen her happy, yes, happy in my arms…but this happiness she wore now, her face bright and light-filled, was a happiness that had never been tainted by deep loss. This was a happiness that was pure, unsullied by darkness and dark times. Her expression was as bright as if she were glowing from within, and though her face was the same, the same face I knew she had, the face I had just kissed and caressed, this one in the dream was a little different. Vampires can't change, so why did she look somehow, impossibly…younger?

"I am awake," I told her with a soft smile, but my voice didn't sound like my own. It was a dream; there would, of course, be some things that are different. But it bothered me…and I couldn't quite put a finger on why it bothered me so very much, my different voice. But it did. I sat up, propping myself onto my elbows, as Kane rose over me, pressing her mouth to mine as she gathered my face in her hands, drawing me to her. She kissed me fiercely, with an energy and rigor that she'd never displayed in front of me before. Kane was very sedate; every move she made was calculated and careful. She expended no energy with her motions, and walked with dignity. And she had dignity here, too…

But she also had excitement. Something that I'd wondered if Kane could even feel.

"Do you forget what day it is?" she asked me mischievously, and then she teased her cool fingers under the edge of the top of my nightgown, drawing the fabric that gave, very easily, down over my breasts. I gasped against her as she lowered her head, as her white-gold hair swept around her shoulders—it was not done up in her usual ponytail, but loose, flowing around her like a waterfall—and her cold mouth found my left breast. She kissed me there passionately, her teeth becoming sharp against me, and when I gazed into her eyes again, I realized they were darkening.

"Not again," I chided her, laughing, shaking my head. "You forget, my love—I am not like you. My human body tires, needs nourishment."

Kane stared down at me, her eyes softening. "I will nourish you," she told me, her voice gruff, her fingers soft against my skin. I closed my eyes, reached up, placed my hand on top of hers and cradled it to my cheek.

"You always do," I told her, the absolute truth. My heart beat quicker inside of me, and I was so full of love at that moment that I was made breathless by it. As I stared up at this woman arching over me, touching me with such tenderness and affection…I felt like I could die, I was so happy.

"What day is it?" I asked her then. Her eyes flicked up to mine, and she smiled against me as she bent her beautiful head back toward my heart.

"It's the day of the Conference," she said.

And somehow, everything…changed.

I was no longer in bed, with Kane on top of me, holding me close. Instead, I was in front of a standing mirror, turning this way and that, looking at my bright red dress and making small adjustments to the little details. The black lace along my creamy shoulders needed to be straightened.

I couldn't quite look at my face, or, at least, I couldn't *see* my face in the mirror. It was surreal as my fingers turned the lace to be the right-side out, and I tried very hard to look at my own reflection…but the mirror was clouded above my shoulders, and there was nothing to be seen.

I heard raised voices, which gave me pause. Had I even heard anything? They sounded so far away and distant…but, yes, there they were again, out in the hallway, raised voices. They sounded so familiar. I turned, lifting up my massive skirts and trying to move through our bedroom toward the door, but it was as if I were moving through quicksand. My breath started coming short, and fear rose through me, thick and black, and when my hand finally closed around the doorknob, I knew that something was very wrong.

The doorknob was hot to the touch. So hot that I screamed.

"Rose? Rose!"

I woke up to someone's hands on my bare shoulders, cold hands so chill that I shuddered beneath their gentle touch, opening my eyes and lifting my arm to block out the glare.

There was a light over the bed, with white-hot

florescent bulbs, and this light was turned on now, shining down on my face so brightly that, for a long moment, I couldn't see clearly. I blinked back the shadows and purple spheres from staring directly into the light, and I looked up at the one shadow that remained.

Kane. Kane sat next to me, gripping my shoulders with tender fingers, staring down at me with a furrowed brow and narrowed eyes, her lips pursed.

"Are you all right?" she whispered to me, letting me go and smoothing an errant strand of hair behind my right ear. She cupped my face gently. "You were screaming." Her eyes, now bright blue, as blue as the sea before an impressive storm, flashed dangerously as she clenched her jaw. "I was in the other room and came back instantly because…because I thought someone was hurting you."

The events of last night slowly started to filter back into my mind. The happy ones—like the fact that Kane and I were finally together, had finally slept together, and it had been magnificent—and the terrible events, too.

Like the fact that two vampires had tried their absolute hardest to kill me.

"No…no one was trying to hurt me," I told her tiredly, sitting up on my elbows and glancing down at my right hand, the one that had reached out to touch the burning-hot doorknob. But of course there was no red welt on my skin, no burn, even though the memory of that white-hot sensation searing into my flesh remained with me, and my hand still pulsed as if it were in pain.

But it had no reason to be in pain.

It was only a dream.

"What happened?" asked Kane, her brow still furrowed.

I blinked and shook my head, smiling softly up at her as I reached across the space between us and took her hand in mine. "I was dreaming. Nothing to worry about. I've been having a lot of strange dreams since coming to the Sullivan Hotel."

Kane's brow furrowed even further. "You have? That's odd, because I have, too, and—"

Kane's room was very large, but even though we were far removed from the door, it was still easy to hear the knock that came upon it; it was so loud and insistent—four hard raps, a beat of time, and then four hard raps again. The knock indicated urgency, as if someone was in trouble. Kane moved off of the bed immediately and walked across the room to open the door.

And that's when all thoughts of last night and of the dream evaporated.

Because when Kane opened the door, standing there in the hallway, her eyes wide, her nostrils flared as she stared into the room at me, lying here on Kane's bed…was Tommie.

I was hoping, selfishly, cowardly, that we were going to have a little more time, just the two of us. Just Kane and me...before the rest of the world came rushing back in and the hard consequences of what we'd done came crashing down on top of us. Just a few more *moments*, even, to get the dust of the dream out of my eyes, to stand up, to kiss Kane good morning. I'd never been able to do that, and I'd wanted to, just once. Once, before the pain I'd caused came into the light.

But karma, as the saying goes, is a bitch. And when Kane opened the door to Tommie, I knew it was time to face the music. It was time to confront exactly what I'd done to her.

No matter how agonizing it was.

I sat up in bed and pulled the sheet to my chest as I saw Kane duck out into the corridor, pulling the door behind her but not really closing it, leaving it slightly ajar as she gripped the doorknob.

And I saw Tommie's face. Just for an instant. Just before the door obscured it.

And it was the face of exquisite pain.

"I was…I was looking for Rose," came Tommie's voice, low and wooden from the hallway. "I couldn't find her anywhere. She was…she was supposed to wait in my rooms for me."

I curled forward onto the bed in pain, crumpling as I heard Tommie's voice behind that half-shut door, the half-shut door that Kane held to her back, still gripping the doorknob in her hand as she shook her head. I could see the side of Kane's body, could see the cascade of her white-blonde hair over her shoulders and back, could see her chin lift, could see the sad contours of her face.

"She was supposed to wait in my rooms so she would stay safe," said Tommie quietly then. And whether she was talking about staying safe from more rogue vampires or from Kane herself, it was impossible to tell. There was so much hurt in her voice, and I put my face in my hands, feeling that pain wash over me like water, absorbing into my skin. I had done this. I had caused this pain—knowingly, willingly.

"Thomasina," said Kane tiredly, and her voice was heavy as she spoke her name. "We need to talk."

There was a long moment of silence, and then: "Let me see her." It was not a question, and the words were forceful, sharp.

Kane shifted her weight. "I don't know if that's—"

My heart in my throat, I clenched the duvet in my hands, and I breathed out. "Kane?" I called. My voice was shaking.

Both women in the corridor fell silent.

"Kane—let Tommie in, please?" I said, and I bit my lip, I closed my eyes, and I tried to dredge up a tiny scrap of courage. I felt so low in that moment. Lower than I'd ever felt in my entire life. Tommie had loved me, loved me fiercely, and I'd done this to her before talking to her about it. Semantics were just that: semantics. Yes, Tommie and I weren't officially dating, but she'd certainly felt that there was something between us, and I had betrayed that trust brutally.

Kane pushed the door open, and she leaned against it with her shoulder, holding it open for Tommie. She didn't look at Tommie, but, rather, she looked into the room at me, working her jaw, her bright blue eyes glittering with something unnameable.

Tommie stood in that open doorway for a long moment, not entering the room, though Kane held the door. She stood there, and she simply breathed, and there was such pain on her face that I was instantly gutted by it. As if I hadn't been gutted already.

"Tommie…" I said, shaking my head, trying to figure out what I could possibly say to make this even a tiny bit better. But I could think of nothing to say, and, in turn, Tommie said nothing, too. She stood still for a moment longer, and then she entered the room. She moved carefully, putting one foot in front of the other as if she were walking on broken glass. She came halfway across the space between us, and then she stopped, balling her hands into fists. There was blood on her white dress shirt. Gwen's blood, I realized. Tommie had taken Gwen into town to get patched up after her accident…effectively letting Kane and I do what we did.

If I'd felt low before, I didn't know how low a person could feel. Tommie had taken Gwen to get stitches, probably; her stomach had been bleeding from a shard of glass from the window, and she'd had a concussion. Tommie had taken care of Gwen *for* me. And then Kane and I had…well…

"You slept with Kane," said Tommie, and there wasn't any inquiry in her tone. She knew, didn't have to ask. Still, she watched me carefully, her jaw clenched, waiting. I took a deep breath, held the comforter over my chest, and I nodded, swallowing.

"Yes," I told her softly. "I did."

Tommie's green eyes flashed brightly with a pain so piercing that I felt it in every part of my body. I felt that pain, and I felt even greater pain for causing that within her.

Tommie lifted her chin, and she breathed out in the stillness. Kane watched the both of us, her jaw clenched tight as Tommie took another step toward me. For another long, painful moment, she said absolutely nothing, only watched me, watched my face, watched my reactions. Tears were already streaking down my cheeks, and now a single tear coursed down Tommie's face, too, a tear that had stood in her clear, green eyes for a long moment before falling. And then Tommie whispered a single word, a single word that broke at the very end of saying it.

"Why?"

There was so much to that simple question, so

much that I couldn't answer right at that moment, nor would I have wanted to. It would have hurt her too much to tell her the deep truth, that Kane and I were meant to be together, that we were deeply in love, that I'd been falling in love with Kane from the first moment that I'd met her. That I cared, so deeply, for Tommie, but that I loved Kane with all my heart, and there was a difference in those two things, and it meant that Tommie and I could never, would never, be together.

And that was too cruel; I could *never* tell her that. So I took a deep breath, feeling the hot tears streak down my face as I searched for softer words…and did the best I could. "I love her," I said to Tommie then, my voice, too, breaking on my words. "I'm so sorry. I love Kane. And I care about you, Tommie. But I love her."

It was as simply put as I could make it, and it was said with as much affection as I had within me, but they were still sharp and hurtful, those words, and I could see the hurt clearly reflected in Tommie's face when she took a single step back, as if I'd punched her with full force in the stomach. There was a haunted look in her eyes, then, and she worked her jaw.

She looked like she was going to say something for the longest moment, as I sat there miserably, but she did not. Instead, Tommie turned away from me, turned and made her way out of the bedroom as quickly as she could possibly go. She brushed past Kane with her shoulder, but it wasn't rough, and I don't think she even meant to do it. Tears were clouding her eyes. Tommie said nothing to her, and then she was out in the hallway, walking away from Kane's bedroom.

I couldn't let her leave—not like this. I needed

to talk to her, to tell her how sorry I was. To try to make this in any way, shape or form…better. I didn't know if I could, but I had to try. I had done a wonderful thing, sleeping with Kane and professing my love for her…but it had consequences, consequences I was now experiencing.

I'd done a terrible thing. And now I had to try my absolute best to fix it. And if it could not be fixed, which I was pretty much assuming it couldn't be…Tommie needed to know how deeply sorry I was for hurting her.

I was completely naked, and I grabbed the closest thing to cover myself with; I pulled the gray, satin sheet under Kane's black duvet out, and I struggled to my feet while simultaneously wrapping myself in the sheet—the kind of thing a drunken frat guy does at a kegger, pretending to wear sheets as togas. But none of it mattered as I raced out of the bedroom, past a silent, pained-looking Kane, into the hallway.

"Tommie, wait!" I called after her. Tommie was already at the corner of the hallway, about to round the bend, but to my surprise—and, perhaps, her own—she stopped. Her back to me was stiff, and her hands were balled into fists at her sides, but she turned a little, her eyes narrowed as she took in my ludicrous costume. I held it tightly about myself, and I padded quietly over the red-and-black tile to her.

"I'm so sorry," I told her, and then I said it a few more times for safe measure. "I am *so* sorry," I whispered, and I gazed at this beautiful woman, this woman who I'd hurt so much, and I watched her expression smooth out, watched her fingers uncurl from their fists. She took one step backward, around the bend, and when I glanced back over my shoulder, I realized that Kane couldn't see around the corner of the hallway. Not that she was watching. She'd gone back into her bedroom to give us some privacy.

Because Kane trusted me wholly. Which was, I realized, pretty damn trusting of her, considering I woke in *Tommie's* bed approximately twenty-four hours earlier.

God, I shouldn't have done that.

I followed Tommie around the corner and watched as she leaned against the wall, tugging a cigarette out of her blood-spattered dress shirt pocket. She lit it up with a silver lighter, pocketing the lighter back into her rear pants pocket with her pale fingers, and she watched me with narrowed, flashing eyes as she took a very long pull on that cigarette.

"You love her," said Tommie, flicking the ash off the end of the cigarette. She blew smoke into the air so that it haloed around her head like light. I nodded, sighing.

"I'm sorry. I should have told you, should have—"

But Tommie held up her hand, shaking her head slowly.

"I knew you loved her," said Tommie simply. "I was just hoping that, with enough time, you could learn to love me, too. And get over her." Her jaw tightened as she jerked her chin back in the direction of Kane's bedroom. "But…something obviously happened," she said, and it came out a little bitterly. "Kane must have told you how she felt."

"Tommie, I'm sorry," I repeated, because I didn't quite know what else to say. I swallowed, tried to find the words, anyway. "That was…that was terrible of me. I should have talked to you before Kane and

I…" I trailed off, because Tommie's flashing eyes told me that she knew exactly what Kane and I had done.

Standing there in the hallway, Tommie's green eyes glittering, my body wrapped in a sheet and absolutely nothing else, I felt a flush come across my cheeks…but Tommie shook her head again, flicking her cigarette with a sharp motion.

"No…it's my fault. I knew you loved Kane," she repeated. "And Kane gets the girl. Again. Because Kane always gets the girl." I paled as I remembered that, once, Tommie had loved Melody with all of her heart. And Melody had chosen Kane over Tommie.

This was history repeating itself. And I was to blame for that.

Tommie shook her head, her eyes pained, dark, and she pushed off from the wall, ready to stalk back down the hallway, but before she could move past me, I reached out, and I took her wrist.

"I don't expect you to forgive me," I told her, my voice cracking. "But I do care about you. As much as it doesn't look like I do right now. And I'm sorry; you don't know how sorry I am. Not that 'sorry' makes anything better…but I care about you, Tommie," I told her, tears leaking out of my eyes.

Tommie paused at that, and when she looked down at me, her own eyes were softer. Gentler. She put the cigarette between her lips, and she raked her other hand back through her hair. She wasn't wearing her trademark hat, and I wondered what had happened to it last night in the fight.

"I care about you, too, Rose," she said, her voice gruff as she glanced away from me, her jaw tightening. "I care about you too much."

I didn't know what else to say. Tommie stayed

where she was, and I stayed, too, my hand gripping her wrist, but softer now.

"It's not your fault," is what Tommie told me then, surprising me. She glanced at me, and her face softened.

"It is. I should have told you first, before anything happened," I said. "Maybe I never should have gone on those dates with you in the first place. I just… I did care about you…and…"

Tommie held up her hand, then sighed when I fell silent. "Those were good memories. I don't regret them."

"I don't, either," I told her truthfully. "I just wish I hadn't hurt you."

"Rose," said Tommie, and she turned, and gently—so gently—she cupped my face in her hands. There was such pain in her own expression, and I stood there tensely, feeling the pain seemingly radiate through her fingertips and into me.

We stood like that, and I felt that pain, and there was nothing I could do to ease it.

After a long moment, Tommie shook her head. And then she said something that twisted a knife deep into me.

"I love you," she said, her voice so soft that I wondered if I'd even heard her speak for half a heartbeat, but I knew exactly what she said when she looked at me…because there was so much pain in her gaze...but there was also love, the exact same type of love that Kane had shown me last night, a love so pure and true and whole that it was more powerful than anything else in the world.

"Rose," Tommie whispered, "I love you, and you don't love me. And that's…that's very sad," she said, struggling with the word while she clenched her jaw, a single tear streaking down her cheek to her chin, then falling away to the red-and-black tile beneath our feet. "And there's nothing that can be done about it," she said. She took a single step back from me, and her hands left my face, falling to her sides.

Tommie watched me for a very long moment. I clenched the sheet in my hands over my heart, wrapped tightly around my body, and I watched her, feeling my heart ache inside of me with a pain so profound that I wanted to weep.

Finally, Tommie straightened, shaking her head again. She lifted her chin, and she gave me the softest, saddest smile.

"Goodbye, Rose," she told me. And then she turned on her heel, and she walked away, sliding her hands into her pockets and curling her shoulders forward as she glided across the floor, walking away from me so quickly that there was soon another bend in the corridor, and she was lost from my sight.

A great sob moved through me then, and I curled forward, putting my face in one hand and trying to hold tightly to the sheet with the other. In a heartbeat, Kane was beside me—perhaps she'd been listening, after all—and she gathered me in her arms, holding me tightly to her. She turned, and, gently, she steered me back to her room. I put one foot in front of the other as I wept, and we were finally at the edge of her bed, and I sat down there stiffly, letting the sheet fall away from me as I folded forward, as I crumpled, putting my face in my hands.

"I hurt her so much," I told her, and I shook my head slowly. "I didn't want to hurt her, and I hurt her so much."

Kane took a deep breath and sat beside me, wrapping a cool arm around me and drawing me to her so that she could hold me gently. We sat like that for a while, until my sobs lessened, until my breathing became easy again.

Then she spoke: "It is just as much my fault as it is yours," she told me, her words soft, coaxing. "Do not be so hard on yourself. You did not make this decision on your own." After a long moment, she took a deep breath and gathered up the corner of the sheet in her hands, gently dabbing it on my cheeks and beneath my eyes, wiping away my tears. "We all hurt others in our lives. None of us is perfect. Life isn't perfect."

"But I didn't mean to," I told her, glancing up at her through my tears. "I didn't *want* to."

"Think about that, then," said Kane then, her face softening. "Isn't that wonderful? Most people don't *want* to hurt each other. They just do, because being human is messy. But very, very few people *want* to hurt. It's just a byproduct of life."

Kane held me tightly and wiped away my tears, and though pain lanced through me, though I felt awful for what I'd done, I stayed in the circle of her arms, and I could feel her love radiating out to me, too, just as much as Tommie's heartache.

And I gripped her arm and held her close, too.

The consequences were being paid.

And still, still, I had Kane.

Love roared through me, moving with the pain.

"I'm assuming that Tommie brought Gwen

back to the Sullivan Hotel with her," Kane told me when she'd finished dressing, adjusting the tie's perfect knot at her throat with her long fingers. She drew her satin hair back over her shoulders and brought it up into the high ponytail at the top of her head, threading an elastic through it. She was watching herself in her floor-length mirror on the inside door of her closet, and I was watching her from my position, seated on the bed. It afforded me the best view…and what a view it was.

But when Kane mentioned Gwen, I straightened, rising from the bed. She flicked her gaze to me and turned, shutting the closet door behind her. "And I'm assuming that you'll want to see her," she told me, one brow raised.

"Immediately." I cleared my throat and smoothed down the front of the unfamiliar skirt that rose out around my hips (it was a very fluffy, vintage-inspired skirt). The outfit that I'd worn yesterday was crumpled on the floor in a somewhat untidy heap. The clothes had blood on them from Gwen, and that wasn't something I thought I should be parading through an entire house full of vampires (how had Tommie done it? I supposed she'd come in through the back, and had just been quiet), so Kane had gone to Dolly's rooms and gotten me a dress and undergarments, promising up and down that, even though Dolly wasn't currently in her rooms, she wouldn't mind in the least if I borrowed a few clothes.

What Kane hadn't gotten me was shoes, because she assumed that I'd wear the ones from yesterday. Which I obviously could—there wasn't anything terribly wrong with them, and they didn't have blood on them, not like my skirt and blouse. But I glanced down at my flats that I'd worn the day before, when Gwen and I had gone to town on what was meant to be such an innocuous errand. Going grocery shopping for the Sullivan Hotel. It was so horrific, the memory of the van accident when we were driving back home, the memory of Gwen bleeding on me, my best friend *bleeding,* and then being hunted, just like me.

The flats I'd worn the day before, incidentally, were covered in mud from the adventurous trek we'd had to take through the woods and along the cliff face, trying to avoid the vampires who were actively hunting us.

The vampires who had tried, last night, to kill us.

But, hey, at least the shoes weren't stained with blood.

"Good. Then you need to go visit your friend," said Kane, adjusting the sleeves of her suit jacket. "And I…I have business to attend to," she said, her nostrils flaring as she breathed out heavily, clenching her jaw. "I need to get to the bottom of who sent those vampires after you. Who wants you dead. And they will be…dealt with."

The way she said *dealt with* was a little bit terrifying. Her voice became so cold suddenly, emotionless and still…as if ice had come to life and had actually spoken. I glanced sidelong at Kane, and she flicked her gaze to me again, immediately softening. "They tried to hurt you," she told me, reaching out and brushing the pad of her thumb alone my jawline. It was such a soft, sensual touch, and I closed my eyes, breathing out as my entire body awoke again from that simple caress. "Whoever sent them… They will pay."

I breathed out, and I nodded as Kane took her

hand from me, turning and adjusting her suit jacket down her front. "Try to stay in Gwen's room until I send Branna for you, all right?" she asked me. She glanced back at me, brows raised, but I was already frowning.

"Why?" I asked, but Kane shook her head.

"I'm sorry, but I don't think being in the Sullivan Hotel is safe for you right now. They sent two vampires to kill you on our *property*. You're not safe, and I need to know that you *are* safe. Just for today," she said softly, stepping closer to me, my front against hers, the skirt of the dress billowing out around her suit pants as we pressed together.

"You're being overprotective," I told her, my mouth turning up at the corners as I wrapped my arms around her. "And I'm going to tell you the truth: I'm not a damsel in distress." I wrapped her suit lapels in my fingers and drew her down to me for a kiss. I paused when she was close enough to touch to me, close enough to kiss, and I looked up into her dazzling blue eyes. "I'm safe here. It's the Sullivan Hotel. No one would dare hurt me here. And I can take care of myself."

That's not something I would have said even a handful of days ago, that I could take care of myself, and that's certainly not something I believed about myself a few months ago, when I felt so fragile that I wondered if Anna's death had removed my desire to live, the very thing that *keeps* one alive, from my heart. Now…now, it was different.

I had dealt with my pain.

I had dealt with losing my lover to a drunk driver, and I had dealt with all of the grief that brings, the aftermath, the scars on my heart that I knew, by now, would never truly heal. I had dealt with falling for Kane, then the rejection that happened afterward. Melody's return. I had dealt with that deep, abiding pain of wanting something so, so desperately and being completely unable to get it, no matter how badly I ached.

There was new pain to deal with, new pain that I had caused Tommie, and that would be worked through, as well. And I knew that I'd be sorry about it my whole life. But that pain, too, had shaped the woman who was standing here right now, gripping a vampire's lapels and drawing her down for the kiss she wanted with her whole heart.

I did want that kiss, and I took it, and Kane gave it gladly, wrapping her arms even tighter about my middle and drawing me to her so that there wasn't a breath of space between us. Her ice-cold mouth was delicious against me; I delighted in it, in her taste and touch, in her tongue.

When I kissed her this morning, there was a languorous about it. The passion was still there, and was rising in me again as I kissed her, but these were kisses that discovered things about Kane, and about myself when kissing her. These were kisses that needed to be slow and sensual, soft and caressing, to learn everything we could about one another. I kissed her, hardly believing this was real. I wanted to pinch myself, I was so happy.

When we both came up for air, Kane looked down at me with a small, sideways smile, but her eyes still bore concern that my kiss could not erase. "Would you humor me?" she asked me then, her voice low, urgent, as she gazed down into my eyes and gripped me softly, spreading her fingers at my waist now and tracing her hands up and down my curves. "Would you wait in Gwen's room for Branna?"

I took a deep breath, and I felt her touch on me, and it felt so good. *She* felt so good, and I loved her so deeply. She didn't ask too much, I knew, especially considering last night. But I was already growing and changing, becoming someone a little bit different from the night before as I stood there in my own shoes and the borrowed dress, pressed tightly to Kane.

"I can take care of myself," I repeated gently, even though I was highly aware that this didn't have any historic precedent for her to believe me. Even though Kane had saved me multiple times, and I was so grateful for her saving me each time, and I loved her, loved her fiercely, the truth of the matter was that I didn't *want* to have to be saved. I wanted to be able to save myself.

And there was no time like the present to learn.

And, really, there was no safer place than the Sullivan Hotel to learn it in.

But relationships are about give and take, and they are most certainly about compromise. And when Kane gazed at me with that poignant expression one last time, pain filling her eyes…I relented.

"Okay," I told her, taking a deep breath. "I'll wait for Branna. But poor Branna… She probably has better things to do with her day than baby-sit a human."

Kane chuckled at that, a beautiful, velvety sound that wrapped me up in its warmth. "We *will* get to the bottom of this sooner, rather than later," Kane promised me, pressing a soft kiss to my forehead, her lips so chill that she made me shiver against her. "I will find out who is behind those hired assassins, and I will make them pay…all before tonight."

"What's tonight?" I asked her playfully, reaching up and placing my arms around her neck, drawing her down to me once more.

"It's the dance," she whispered, before she kissed me again.

The dance. That's right; Gwen had told me about it. A dance that the entire town was invited to—vampires and humans mingling together.

What could possibly go wrong?

Kane backed away, and a small smile turned her mouth up at the corners again. I hadn't had the pleasure of seeing Kane smile often before now, but I was beginning to realize that whenever she smiled at me, my love for her grew even more: bigger, brighter, truer.

God, she looked so beautiful when she smiled. Devastatingly so. The layers of sadness that always seemed to exist around Kane Sullivan melted away in those moments, revealing the woman beneath all of it. The woman she had once been, and the woman she was changing into again.

"Go to Gwen," she told me, brushing a kiss to each cheek and squeezing my shoulders as she stepped back. "Talk with her, make sure she is well, and before you know it, I will send Branna along, and then you can go get breakfast. Unless you want to go to the kitchens first with me now?"

"Gwen's much more important than a little hunger," I told her, slipping on my muddy shoes. I didn't even have time to wipe them off or wash them; I was too anxious to see Gwen and make absolutely sure she was all right.

Kane ushered me to Gwen's door, through the floors and corridors of the Sullivan Hotel. Gwen's rooms were right next to mine, so I'd be able to duck in for a quick change of clothes soon, anyway. I stood up on my tiptoes to kiss Kane goodbye, and I locked eyes with her for a long moment.

"*You* be safe, okay?" I asked her, my brow furrowed as I smoothed her lapels down, smoothed the shoulders of her suit jacket, my fingers lingering. "Just…be careful."

"Always," she promised me, her voice low as she brushed her lips against my forehead one last time, and then she was clicking back down the corridor, her shoes resounding smartly off the tiled floor. My eyes lingered on that beautiful, white-blonde ponytail that swayed over her shoulders until she disappeared around the corner.

I cleared my throat, then, and I turned back to Gwen's room, and I knocked on the door.

"Who is it?" croaked Gwen from inside. She sounded testy, which made me happy. A testy Gwen meant that she was probably mostly okay.

I hoped.

"It's me, Gwen," I told her, my voice low as I leaned close to the door. "Can I come in?"

"Yes," she snapped, and I frowned a little as I turned the doorknob…but it was locked.

"Just a minute," I heard, and then I heard, too, a shuffle, and a *click* as she unlocked the door. And then the sound of wood scraping against wood, like she was moving a piece of furniture in her room.

When Gwen opened that door to me, she opened it just a tiny bit, and she peered out through the crack suspiciously, with one eye. It was a very narrowed, unhappy eye, and when she made certain that it was definitely me standing there, she yanked the door open the whole way, took one step out, grabbed my arm and all but pulled me into the room after her, before throwing the door closed again and locking it immediately.

And then she took one of the chairs from her little table next to her kitchenette, and she tucked the back of the chair beneath the doorknob, effectively barricading the door.

When Gwen turned to look back at me, yes, she looked pale from her loss of blood.

But she also looked like she'd just seen a ghost.

"Are you okay?" she asked me, stepping forward and gripping my shoulders tightly before turning even *paler* when she saw the healing wounds on my neck. "Oh, my God," she muttered, taking a step back then, staring at me as if I'd become a different person. She picked up one of the heavy silver candlesticks from the little table beside the door, and she actually brandished it at me. "Are you one of them?" she hissed.

One of them.

A vampire.

I stared at my best friend, still holding the candlestick like a club. I guess the cat was out of the bag now. How did she know that that's what had hunted us last night? But it didn't matter. She needed to know the truth, and I probably shouldn't have kept the truth from her in the first place.

"I'm not anything but me, Gwen," I told her quietly, putting up my hands in a "I surrender" sort of pose. "Are you…are you all right?"

Gwen snorted, and in that moment, she looked

and acted exactly like my best friend—not a lady holding a candlestick as if she was going to beat me up with it. "No," she said then, the testiness coming through her voice loud and clear. "I'm not all right. I had to get stitches in my belly, and I remember some pretty weird shit from last night, Rose."

I lifted my brows and stared at her. "Do you know?" I asked then.

"Know that we're living in a house full of fucking vampires? Yeah. I know," she muttered, and she set the candlestick back down on the table heavily. "Please tell me you're not one of them," she said, and the words came out sounding weary. "Because, seriously, I don't think I could take it. And my box of wooden stakes hasn't arrived from Amazon Prime yet," she quipped. Though her voice was tired when she said it, her eyes flashed with that familiar fire.

"I'm not a vampire," I promised her, my voice gentle, and then Gwen nodded once, did a little uncharacteristic, nervous laugh, and walked quickly over to me. She gripped me so tightly in a hug that I felt all of the air squeezed out of my lungs.

"I didn't think you were," she said, sniffing as she pillowed her chin on my shoulder, "but I don't know. It's been a *really* weird twenty-four hours, Rose. So, you know, I just wanted to make sure."

"Anyway, even if I *was* a vampire, I think silver is effective against werewolves, not vampires," I joked, jerking my thumb to the candlestick and taking a step back. I held Gwen out at arm's length and took in her appearance. God, she looked positively ragged. "What do you remember from last night?" I asked her seriously.

"Oh, you know…someone running Moochie

off the side of the road," Gwen said, pronouncing her van's name as if she were mourning a good friend. And she might be; I didn't really get to pay much attention to the damage that van had sustained in the accident, but I was kind of wondering if Moochie could be resurrected from that level of death. "I remember…" Gwen frowned a little, shaking her head. "Not much. But I remember there being people with sharp teeth attacking the both of us, and when I asked Tommie about it, she said they were all vampires. So..."

"Tommie told you that?" I asked, my brows up.

"Yeah. She said that since you and she were an item now, it was important that I knew the truth," said Gwen, crossing her arms in front of her. Now it was her turn to raise her brows. "So…did *you* know they were vampires?"

I bit my lip, and then I nodded. "Yes. I'm sorry. I didn't think it'd be good to tell you. There are treaties in place," I said, lifting my hand before Gwen could start yelling at me, "so I thought you'd be safe, and I thought it'd be better if you didn't know, so you wouldn't worry."

"Worry," Gwen repeated the two syllables as if they were some kind of joke. "Rose, those vampires last night almost killed the both of us. Like, actual, one hundred percent *murder*. We'd be dead right now if Tommie and Kane hadn't come along to save our asses."

I shifted my weight on my feet and crossed my own arms, feeling a touch uncomfortable. "Yeah. It was really wonderful of the both of them," I told her, and then Gwen regarded me curiously.

"Something happened," she said, and she lifted her arms in the air, shaking her head. "Rose, I love you, but you can tell me all about it while you help me finish packing." And then she stepped to the side, and I could see what her body had been hiding this whole time. On top of her bed's coverlet, there was an open suitcase.

Gwen was packing her clothes.

"You're leaving?" I asked her, because I wasn't entirely sure (and a large part of me couldn't believe it), but Gwen's guilty look when she glanced my way again confirmed it. "Gwen, you can't go," I told her, rushing over to her bed and standing in front of the suitcase, holding out my arms, as if *that* could stop her. Gwen glanced at me and sighed, biting her lip.

"We live in a house full of vampires. Don't you have any self-preservation in you at all? Like, not even a little?" asked Gwen plaintively. "I mean, seriously, two of those asshole vampires almost *killed* you last night, and you want to remain in a house absolutely *infested* with them?"

"You don't... You don't understand," I said, thinking as quickly as I could. "They're not *all* like that. Kane and Tommie and the rest of them, they're not—"

"Look, I know you have feelings for Tommie," Gwen said, too quickly for me to interject, "and that's all nice and good. But if you have feelings for this one, you can have feelings for someone else. There are definitely other ladies out there who *aren't* vampires, women who would actually be *good* for you—"

"Kane's good for me," I told her, and Gwen stopped speaking to stare at me, her mouth actually falling open.

"Kane," she said then, her voice deadpan.

"Kane," I repeated, straightening a little "Last night. Kane and I got together last night."

"What about Tommie?" asked Gwen, putting her hands on her hips. "Do you know how much that poor woman loves you? I mean, she's not a big talker, but she talked to me about it a little, just to pass the time on the ride to and from the doctor's, and let me tell you, she's absolutely crazy for you."

"That…rubs a little bit of salt in my wounds," I admitted, wincing, "and, yes, Tommie knows about it. And, no, it didn't go over that well. And, *yes,* I feel absolutely terrible about the fact that I hurt Tommie, and I've never been sorrier for anything in my entire life. But Kane and I…we're meant to be together, Gwen. It's just…it's something that's…" I trailed off, searching for the right word, and miraculously, the perfect one came to me: "Fated. We're fated," I repeated, my voice low as I realized exactly how true that was. I felt it in my bones, that word. *Fated.*

Gwen stared at me for a long moment, and slowly her expression became hard and stony, her mouth shifting into a thin, hard line. "That's sweet, honey. I'm happy for you. But you've got to know you can't stay here."

"What?" I spluttered as Gwen moved past me, angling toward her dresser. She opened the top drawer, and she removed a stack of shirts and turned on her heel, stalking over the bed to dump them into the suitcase. "What are you talking about?" I asked, as Gwen sailed past me again, intent on another stack of clothes from the drawer.

"Tommie said that those vampires last night? They were after *you.* Which means that you're not safe here," she said crisply. "You know that as well as I do."

"I don't *know* that," I told her, crossing my arms

in front of myself tightly. "And Kane told me that she was getting to the bottom of it right now. That she was going to find the person responsible for all of this."

Gwen cast me a withering look. "How do you know there was only one? There wasn't one last night; there were *two*. *Two* vampires who were trying to kill us. How do you know that *any* vampire is good? They're bloodsuckers. I mean, almost every time vampires comes up in anything—books, movies—they're not *good,* honey. They're evil. They tried to *kill* us."

"*Not the Sullivans,*" I promised her, holding up hands again in protest. "The Sullivans would never do anything to harm us, Gwen—"

And at that, Gwen rounded on me. She tossed her last stack of shirts into the suitcase, and she came almost nose to nose with me, her eyes flashing dangerously. "Then who the hell," she said, her voice in a growl, "bit your neck?"

I put my hand over my healing wounds self-consciously and took a step back.

Tommie must have told her.

"Mags," I said the word quietly, lifting my chin and holding her gaze. "Mags…did this."

"Mags *Sullivan,*" said Gwen, but when she spread her hands triumphantly, she didn't look all that triumphant; she looked exhausted. "Look, Rose, I can't force you to do anything," she muttered, moving past me and yanking another dresser drawer open. "But I'm your best friend, and I'm telling you right now, being at the Sullivan Hotel isn't safe for either one of us. And I'm getting the hell out of Dodge. And I'm really, really hoping you'll recognize what's good for you, too, and that you'll come with me."

She grabbed a couple of pairs of jeans from the

dresser and stuffed them in her suitcase. That's when she stopped and stood next to me, breathing out into the stillness with an exasperated sigh. "So? What's it gonna be? Are you going to come with me?" she prompted, searching my face.

"Gwen…" I began, but she was already moving past me, back toward the dresser.

"I knew it. I knew you wouldn't come with me," she muttered, grabbing a few more pairs of jeans out of the dresser, shoving the empty drawer closed with her bottom. "Have they put you under a spell or something?" she asked, and she was being perfectly serious when she glanced at me in frustration.

"That's probably witches you're thinking of," I said, joking weakly, but Gwen flashed me another angry look and tossed the rest of the jeans into her suitcase.

"That's not funny, and you know it," she muttered. Then she stepped back from the suitcase and looked down at the overly full thing. And that's when I realized she was done packing. There was nothing left in the room for her to pack. Gwen didn't own much; she liked to be "as free as a bird," as she'd always told me, and everything she owned was capable of fitting into her vintage blue suitcase.

And it was full now.

"You're leaving…today?" I asked her, and she nodded, but she wouldn't look at me as she snapped the suitcase shut, pushing down on the latches a little harder than necessary to force them closed.

"I don't feel safe here, honey. And you shouldn't, either," she said, finally turning to face me. "Please come with me?"

I stared at my best friend, my best friend who had gotten me this job at the Sullivan Hotel in the first place, my best friend who had convinced Kane to hire me on, sight unseen, without a resume. Gwen had been the one to set everything in motion; Gwen had been the one to break me out of my sadness about Anna, to convince me that I needed a fresh start, or I would be haunted by her forever. Gwen had been the one to push me out of my comfort zone, to bring me here, to Eternal Cove.

Gwen had changed my life irrevocably, had been my best friend for so long…and now, we were being separated again.

I couldn't leave Kane, not when something had just started between us. Not when we were falling in love. And I couldn't leave Tommie—not like this.

Gwen knew all of that when she looked at my face. She knew, and she didn't say anything else, only stepped forward and wrapped her arms around my shoulders, holding me close.

"I'm going to miss you," she said simply, squeezing me tight. "It was really great living together again, even if it was only for a couple of days. We haven't done anything like that since college. It was nice," she said, and she sounded wistful as she took a step back, as she gazed at me with sad eyes. "I hope you're going to be okay, honey. I'm really worried about you. I wish there was something I could say to convince you to come with me."

"I'm sorry, Gwen," I told her, and I really was.

This seemed to be the morning of apologies.

And of goodbyes.

Gwen shrugged a little, as if to shake the sadness away. Then she chuckled, but it sounded strained. "So, I'm all packed. You know I pack light," she said, sniffing, and when she turned away from me, I could see that there were unshed tears in her eyes. "So, I guess I go down and hike to where Moochie's beached… Poor guy. It's not that far from the Sullivan Hotel. And then I'll see what it takes to get a tow truck out to the middle of nowhere," she muttered, snatching up her cell phone from the top of the dresser and sliding it into her back jeans pocket.

"Don't leave yet," I told her, and she glanced at me quickly, but I raised my hands. "Wouldn't it be easier to call a tow truck place from here? That way, you could figure out where you're towing it to, look it up first. I mean, have you even had breakfast yet?"

Gwen wrinkled her nose. "Since Tommie just hauled my ass from the doctor's to here just a little while ago…no. That's not something that was on the morning agenda."

"Okay," I told her with a resolute smile. "You call the towing company and a garage or something. Figure out where you're going to take Moochie and how much it's going to cost. I'll go down to the kitchens and get us both something to eat. I'll bring it right back. What do you want?"

Gwen glanced at me suspiciously, as if she was trying to figure out if this was an elaborate ploy to get her to stay, but then her expression softened. "Like…a million scrambled eggs. And a couple of cinnamon buns. And if she has pancakes, some of those. And if she doesn't have pancakes, some waffles. Hell, even if she *does* have pancakes, some waffles, too, okay? And don't forget syrup, because you can't eat any of that without syrup." She grinned at me as I turned, about to make my way back toward the door. "Thanks, Rose," she said, her voice soft.

"Don't mention it," I told her, grinning back

over my shoulder.

I slipped out of her rooms, and I shut the door behind me. Already, I could hear her locking it and sliding the chair beneath the doorknob. I was a little shaken. I guess it was ridiculous to think that my best friend didn't fear anything, but, honestly, in all the time I'd known her…she really hadn't ever been afraid. Not once. This was the woman who said she'd buy a ticket to ride to the moon the second NASA ever made rocket buses. This was the woman who completely uprooted her life and moved whenever and wherever the wind took her. Even during all of our late-night talks, where we discussed everything, where we got to the deepest, darkest parts of ourselves…the only thing she'd ever told me she was afraid of was some idiot becoming president and pushing the nuclear button for no reason.

That was it. And I knew it was the truth, because I knew Gwen like the back of my hand.

But this…this accident last night, and being hunted…it had done something to her, changed her.

And that made my heart ache.

To say that I wasn't afraid wouldn't be exactly true. I was afraid. But I just didn't care anymore. I'd been through enough already. If another vampire came at me, he'd have hell to deal with.

And that was the honest truth.

So I was walking down the hallway, worrying about Gwen…but I was not remembering something very important. In fact, I was blissfully unaware at that moment that, very recently, I'd promised Kane that I would wait for Branna in Gwen's rooms. I had promised that I would not, under any circumstances, wander the corridors alone.

But, in my shock over Gwen deciding to leave, I'd honestly forgotten my promise. And I walked the hall, thinking hard about Gwen, about Tommie, about Kane…about a million different things…

Until my reverie was broken by someone singing.

I was in a hotel that was almost full to capacity, so hearing someone else's voice shouldn't have been so startling. But I was also on the floor that had been converted to apartments for the hotel's staff. And all of the staff had been deployed today, considering that we were full up at the hotel. Every single person was working, according to the schedule. But, as I stood there, my entire body tense, I knew that even with everyone working, there could have been a million reasons that I was hearing singing.

But none of those million reasons ran through my head at that moment.

Because my body reacted to the singing long before my head could come up with any sort of coherent thought.

All of the hairs on the back of my neck were standing on end. It was the strangest thing, as if I'd just seen something terrifying, or heard something terrifying, but, no—it was just a pleasant female voice, humming something softly. It wasn't a necessarily scary sound, but for some reason…it unnerved me.

I stood still for a long moment, trying to get my bearings. Where was the humming coming from? That's when I noticed the big, oaken door to my right, the one with the black painted border, standing slightly open. It was the last door on the floor before the enormous staircase.

It was no big deal, obviously, that the door was

ajar; someone must just be in there, probably a fellow staffer cleaning up the room because they needed it for a guest, since we were so full. But as I walked past the door, I paused, because I saw someone in the room.

Someone I didn't recognize.

I shouldn't have stared, but an odd sensation overwhelmed me. The woman in the mirror…she looked so familiar. Like the kind of familiar that makes your brain stretch and strain as you try, desperately, to remember where you saw her before. Because you know that you *have* seen her, have met her, have spoken with her…but, for the life of you, you can't remember when or where or why.

I stood there in the hallway, as still as a statue, and I peered through the open crack of the door at the woman standing just inside. The room was similar in layout to the ones that Gwen and I had, save for one glaring difference. There was no furniture in it. Nothing at all except for the tall, antique standing mirror that was positioned along the opposite wall. This is what the woman was standing in front of. Her back was to me, but I could see her reflection in the mirror clearly.

She was tall, and she was very pale. I noticed that first, and I realized that the person I was looking at must be a vampire. Not that a human being can't be pale, but this woman was *deathly* pale, ashen pale…vampire pale. After meeting and knowing enough vampires, I knew vampire pale when I saw it.

She stood in front of the mirror, and she ran her fingers through her long, blonde hair. It was the color of wheat and rolled in waves down her back as she threaded her fingers through it, combing it. She was staring at herself in the glass and humming something quietly to herself. Honestly, I'm surprised I had even heard her voice out in the corridor; it was that soft.

She had very high cheekbones and big blue eyes. She was very pretty, but there was something about her that was just a little…off. It made me shiver as I stood there, watching her. She was wearing a color of lipstick that was bright, cherry red, and it contrasted with the white of her incisors sharply, though it complemented her red dress.

Where had I seen that red dress before? It looked almost as familiar to me as her face did.

As I watched, the woman did a little turn in the mirror, and she hummed a little bit louder. When she glanced at her reflection, a smile turned her mouth up at the corners, and it wasn't mischievous or charming; it was downright *evil.*

And then, just at that moment, she stopped humming. She stood straight and tall as she gazed at her reflection, and she sighed, again running her fingers over her hair.

"Soon," she whispered, and she glanced at her reflection, smiling at it. She blew her own likeness a kiss, and then she stepped closer to the mirror. She pressed her cherry-red mouth to the glass, and when she stepped back again, a kiss print appeared on the mirror's surface.

My eyes were clamped to her reflection, because when she took a step back from the mirror, she...well...

She *changed.*

She ran her fingers over her hair again, and the strands transformed from long, wheat-colored waves to large bloodred curls that cascaded over her shoulders. And when she put her red-painted fingernails over her face, as if she were playing an eerie game of hide-and-seek, my heart was in my throat.

The woman removed her hands from her face with a flourish, and she grinned wickedly at her own reflection in the mirror.

I stared at her, and I took a step backward, the world reeling beneath me.

Because it was Melody standing there in that empty bedroom.

This woman had just transformed into Melody.

*...to be continued*

Who is Melody, and is she capable of keeping Rose and Kane apart? Experience this epic romance as it unfolds in the seventh Sullivan Vampire story, *Eternal Dream*, coming soon!

Made in the USA
San Bernardino, CA
09 September 2019